JOE and the Race to Rescue

JOE and the Race to Rescue

VICTORIA EVELEIGH

Illustrated by Chris Eveleigh

Orion
Children's Books

First published in Great Britain in 2014
by Orion Children's Books
a division of the Orion Publishing Group Ltd
Orion House
5 Upper St Martin's Lane
London WC2H 9EA
An Hachette UK Company

1 3 5 7 9 10 8 6 4 2

A catalogue record for this book
is available from the British Library.

ISBN 978 1 4440 0759 6

Printed in Great Britain by
Clays Ltd, St Ives plc

www.orionbooks.co.uk

For my godson, Max,
who enjoys writing stories too.

Chapter 1

J oe and Martin sat in the back seat of the car, too busy chatting to take much notice of the familiar scenery as it flicked by. They usually travelled this route together on the school bus, but today the journey had a carefree holiday feel about it. Nigel, Martin's dad, was driving them to the National Ploughing Championships, which were taking place on a farm near their local town of Bellsham.

Watching fields being ploughed wouldn't have been high on Joe's list of cool things to do at half term when he was living in Birmingham, but his life had changed a lot since then. His family had moved to Newbridge Farm, Mum had given up teaching and turned the farm into a horse sanctuary, and he'd developed new interests like riding and fishing.

"Nearly there," Nigel said, grinning. He'd suggested the day out because he loved vintage tractors.

It was the horse-drawn ploughing that Joe really wanted to see. He'd encountered heavy horses for the first time at the Horse of the Year Show a few weeks ago, but he'd been too busy riding Lightning in the Bellsham Vale mounted games team to do more than admire them from afar. This would be a great opportunity to see some at close quarters.

He glanced at his watch: nearly midday. Emily would be taking Lightning to the Pony Club rally.

It was hard to accept he'd grown out of his pony. They'd done really well, and she'd taught him so much, but now she belonged to his little sister and they both seemed perfectly happy together. Adapting to a new pony wasn't turning out to be so easy for him, but he didn't want to think about that right now. An afternoon of enjoyment lay ahead, with no expectations or pressure. After a hectic year of competitions it would be a treat to be a spectator for a change.

Nigel pulled into a large grassy field and parked next to the car they'd been following. More cars lined up beside them – row upon row – a bizarre temporary crop glinting in the October sunshine. The fields beyond were filled with marquees, tents, arenas and lorries. Brown patches of earth, like vast strips of sticking plaster, alternated with areas that hadn't been ploughed yet.

Nigel paid at the entrance gate and headed to where the vintage tractors were working. Martin followed. Joe looked wistfully through the open gate of a field signposted *Working Horses,* then hurried to catch up.

The three of them stood for a long time watching some grey Ferguson tractors at work, while Nigel talked enthusiastically about how they had transformed farming. It was odd to think that less than a hundred years ago they'd been cutting-edge. They looked like toys compared with modern farm machinery.

Eventually they moved on to look at the others: blue and orange Fordson Majors, green Field Marshalls with huge exhaust pipes, red and white McCormick International Harvesters, bright yellow Caterpillar crawlers . . . Nigel bombarded the boys with information about each one.

"Hey, how are you doing? I haven't seen you for ages!" A tall man with dark hair and a beard stopped to talk to Nigel. It sounded as if the conversation was going to be a long one. Joe wondered whether he'd ever get to see the horses at this rate.

To his relief, Martin caught his eye and pointed towards the refreshment tent. He nodded in reply.

Martin tapped his dad on the shoulder. "We're going to get something to eat. Okay?"

"Fine. Got that money I gave you?" Nigel replied.

Martin patted his pocket and nodded.

"Be by the entrance at five o'clock," Nigel said, and turned his attention back to an in-depth discussion about tractors.

Lunch was fried bacon in a large white bun, a packet of crisps, a can of fizzy drink and a double ice-cream cone with a chocolate flake in it – not exactly healthy eating, but never mind. It was great to be able to have junk food again once in a while. When Joe and Lightning had been in the Pony Club games team together, he'd grown so much taller that he'd had to be really careful about keeping within the weight limit for her size.

Joe and Martin sat on a straw bale and finished their ice-creams. The weather seemed hotter than it had been all summer.

"D'you mind going to see the horses next?" Joe asked.

"Dad put you off tractors for life?" Martin grinned. "Reminds me of a joke."

Joe groaned. "Why am I not surprised?" Martin had an inexhaustible supply of jokes – some better than others. "Go on, then."

"What do you call someone who used to like tractors?"

"Er . . . Haven't a clue."

"An extractor fan!" Martin said triumphantly. "Ex-tractor fan. Get it?"

Joe couldn't help smiling. "Terrible." He got up and stretched. "Come on, let's go and see some real horsepower."

Dry stubble scrunched underfoot as the two friends walked towards the area where the ploughing was taking place. Even from a distance the horses grabbed Joe's attention. He couldn't explain why, but he always felt irresistibly drawn to them.

"Mind your backs, please!"

Joe looked round to see a couple of huge horses marching towards him, their great dinner-plate hooves thudding on the ground. He stood, mesmerised. They looked magnificent, adorned with brightly coloured ribbons and polished horse brasses.

Martin grabbed Joe's arm and pulled him out of the way.

The Shires – at least Joe guessed that was what they were – came so close that the air trembled as they passed by, their harness clinking like armour. They were even larger than Joe had imagined – not just taller but bulkier as well. Four of Lightning's legs put together wouldn't have been as thick as one of theirs.

In spite of the warm weather, the man driving them wore a woollen suit and a shirt and tie. "Thank you. Much obliged!" he called, turning briefly to smile at the boys. Round-rimmed glasses magnified his wrinkled eyes, giving him the look of a wise old owl wearing a tweed cap.

They fell into step behind him without saying a word. Joe followed as closely as he could, and tried to imagine what it would be like to drive such massively powerful creatures.

Like all good horsemen, the man made it look effortless. A quiet word or chirruping noise seemed to be all that was needed to guide them: "Velvet, steady, there's a girl," or "Sherman, *chlik chlik*, good lad."

So Velvet's the black one, and she's a mare, Joe said to himself. She's the trickier of the two, by the looks of it. The dappled grey's called Sherman, and he's a "lad". I expect he's a gelding because he seems too laid back to be a stallion. I wonder whether they're related. Perhaps I'll ask . . . Maybe it's dangerous to talk to someone when they're driving, though . . . I wonder why the reins are like thin white ropes when the rest of the harness is all brown leather and brass . . . And I wonder why their tails are plaited up like that, with those ribbons and funny dart-like things in them. They've got darts and ribbons in their manes too – much more fun than the plain little plaits we have to do at Pony Club.

As Velvet and Sherman lifted each hoof off the ground with a swirl of feathery white hairs, their broad horseshoes glinted in the sunlight.

My wishing shoe must have looked like that when it was new. The thought took Joe by surprise; he'd almost forgotten about the rusty old horseshoe hidden in a box under his bed. Joe had dug it up soon after they'd arrived at Newbridge Farm, in the field that Mum now used as her kitchen garden. It was hard to remember how different things had been then.

Nellie, their neighbour and good friend, was the only person who knew about Joe's horseshoe. She'd seen him dig it up, and it was she who'd suggested making it into a wishing shoe with a wish rolled up on a piece of coloured paper in each of the seven

7

holes. Nellie was Romany, and wishing shoes were a Romany tradition, apparently. The weird thing was that it really had helped, or so it seemed . . .

He'd wished for a dog, and Rusty had come along. His wish that Mum would get better after falling off Lady had definitely come true. She'd made a full recovery, and she and Lady were getting along fine now. He'd made a wish to go home – meaning Birmingham – but pretty soon he'd realised he felt more at home at Newbridge Farm, so that had worked out in an unexpected way. His wish for friends had been successful – he'd never had so many. Martin had become his best mate, of course, and Caroline was a good friend as well. He liked her *a lot*, though, and that made it sort of complicated.

What else? That wish for good energy had been a slightly strange one, but he had to admit his whole outlook on life had become much more positive since he'd made his wishes, and great things had followed on from that, so perhaps there really was such a thing as good energy.

Most bizarre of all, he'd written down "Fortune" as a wish, hoping for lots of money to appear from somewhere, but a pony called Fortune had turned up instead. It was true that she wasn't exactly living up to expectations at the moment, but he'd only had her a few weeks. Perhaps, as far as the wish was concerned, it had kept its part of the bargain and wasn't responsible for how Fortune turned out; maybe that was up to Joe.

Yes, it seemed that six out of seven wishes had come true so far. The final one, "England team", had been way too ambitious from the start. He'd been football-crazy at the time but riding had taken over since then, so getting into the England team was even less likely to happen now.

"Whoa!" the man said to his horses. They stopped instantly. Joe and Martin ground to a halt too. They'd arrived at the ploughing plots.

Several people immediately hurried over and started talking. Joe longed to find out more about the horses, but it was embarrassing hovering in the background so the two boys moved away to take a look at the other participants.

Joe was used to Pony Club events, where there were strict dress and turnout codes and everything was highly organised. Here, everything seemed much more relaxed, with ploughmen working the plots in their own time and frequently pausing to adjust their machinery or give their horses a rest. Some of the competitors were dressed smartly but others, especially the younger ones, wore jeans, T-shirts and baseball caps. The appearance of the horses also varied, from a few immaculately turned out pairs like

Velvet and Sherman to dusty-coated animals wearing dull working harness.

The air smelled of fresh earth and autumn. Murmured words and the clinking of the ploughs as they turned the soil were punctuated by other gentle sounds like horses blowing through their noses. In this field there weren't any engines popping away or smoky fumes wafting from hot exhaust pipes.

Joe looked back at Sherman and Velvet, keen for an opportunity to go and talk to their owner. There was only one person there now. He appeared to be helping to adjust the plough. It looked like a serious, skilful business. The horses stood quietly with their heads together, temporarily off duty.

"That's unusual, isn't it?" Martin said, pointing towards two stocky light brown horses with smooth legs, barrel-shaped bodies and long raffia plaits in their manes.

"Yup, smart, aren't they?" Joe said. "I think they're Suffolk Punches." He'd been reading about the breed the other day in Emily's pony magazine. "They're very rare, and their colour is officially 'chesnut' without a 't' in the middle."

"Not the *horses*," Martin said. "The person behind them."

Joe looked, and saw a middle-aged woman with an outdoorsy no-nonsense face holding the plough. She wore a tweed cap, checked shirt, baggy brown trousers and stout leather boots, so it was easy to miss the fact she was female. "Oh, I see what you mean – it's a woman!" he said much too loudly.

"Ssshh, you idiot!" Martin hissed, and they both started laughing.

All of a sudden Joe realised the other reason why this felt so different from Pony Club competitions: most of the people here were male. For once it felt completely normal to be a boy who loved horses.

Joe glanced over to where the Shires had been standing, but they weren't there any more. They were down at the other end of the plots, ploughing. "Come on, let's go and watch Velvet and Sherman working," he said to Martin.

"*Who?*"

"The Shire horses we walked behind," Joe said impatiently. How could Martin have avoided noticing what they were called? The man had said their names often enough.

By the time the boys reached the plot, Velvet and Sherman had turned and were walking steadily towards them, their ears swivelling to pick up instructions and words of encouragement from the ploughman. Joe watched, fascinated, as Sherman made his way along the furrow, placing his huge hooves in front of each other with careful precision, barely grazing the soil on either side. The horses were particularly beautiful now. Their necks were arched and they had a look of concentration on their faces as they worked. The ground they'd already ploughed had long, uniform waves of earth piled neatly against each other, as straight as a ruler.

How have those two gigantic animals learned to be that accurate? Joe wondered. There's so much I want to find out. Being a spectator's okay, but I'd love to be the one behind that plough.

Chapter 2

Rusty bounded out of the stable barn, whining with excitement, and a few moments later there was the sound of Chris' van driving into the yard.

"How does he know?" Emily asked from Lightning's stable.

"ESP," Joe replied.

"What?"

"Extrasensory perception. Nellie often talks about it. She says it's a sixth sense that animals feel, but a lot of humans ignore it."

Nellie knew a lot about animals. Joe often felt she had a sixth sense, especially when it came to horses.

"Why do we ignore our sixth sense, if it's so useful?" Emily asked.

Joe leaned on Lightning's stable door. "I don't know. Perhaps it's because we've lost touch with nature, or we're taught not to believe in things that can't be explained. Why do you always ask so many questions?"

Emily gave him a radiant smile. "Because I have an enquiring mind. It's a sign of superior intelligence."

"Wrong," Joe said triumphantly. "If you were intelligent you'd know the answers anyway."

Emily stuck her tongue out – a sure sign of defeat.

Just at that moment Chris walked into the barn, a delighted Rusty by his side. "Hi there. Which ones today?"

Joe took charge. "Lightning, ET and Bubble and Squeak need trims; Fortune needs shoeing. Mum says the others will be okay for a couple of weeks. Oh, she also said watch out for Tyler." He pointed to a handsome chestnut in a stable at the far end of the barn.

"He's nice. Why's he here?"

"Debbie – you know, Debbie who teaches at Pony

Club – was given him by someone who couldn't cope. Mum agreed she could keep him here in return for helping to exercise the horses, but I think she's beginning to regret it. He's got more problems than the rehabs."

"Oh?"

"He's got sharp teeth and he knows how to use them."

"Kicks as well," Emily said.

"Delightful," Chris commented.

"Can you do Lightning first?" Emily asked. "Caroline's coming soon; we're going out for a ride."

Caroline was Chris' stepsister. She was in the same year as Joe at school and they'd become especially close since they'd ridden in the Prince Philip Cup team together. She and Emily got on well too, despite a gap of nearly three years.

Chris went into Lightning's stable and lifted each of her legs in turn. "Not much to do here. Her hooves are in pretty good shape. I'll balance them a bit, and you'll be free to go."

"Amazing, considering all the work she's had recently," said Joe. He'd wanted to give her a holiday after the Horse of the Year Show, but Emily – overjoyed that Lightning was now hers – had started to ride her straight away.

"Most unshod hooves thrive on hard work, as long as nutrition and everything are spot on," Chris said.

Soon he'd finished seeing to Lightning. "Fortune next?" he asked Joe. "If I hurry you'll be able to join the girls on their ride."

Joe hesitated. "I'd better not. Mum's gone to Landsdown Farmers for feed and things, so I should probably stay here."

Rides with Caroline were much more fun than normal ones around the roads and bridleways because her dad owned a huge farm. Part of Joe longed to join the girls, but at the same time he was surprisingly glad of an excuse to stay behind. Fortune was turning out to be far more complicated and difficult to control than he'd hoped. It had been easy to feel good on Lightning, but Fortune made him wary and tense. It didn't help that everyone kept telling him how lucky he was to have such a gorgeous-looking champion Prince Philip Cup pony. He imagined people saying things like "she's too much for him" and "he only did well with Lightning because she's such a wonderful, forgiving pony", and he knew they'd be right.

"Would you like a cup of tea, Chris?" Emily asked.

He'd already set to work on Fortune, removing her shoes. "Thought you'd never ask. White, no sugar, thanks."

"White, no sugar coming up," Emily said, and went off to the house.

"Beautiful, hard hooves," Chris said, pulling off another shoe. "She'd be fine barefoot, if you'd like to try."

"Better not," Joe replied. "One of the many things in her loan agreement is that she's shod at least every six weeks. Mrs McCulloch's unbelievably fussy about Fortune: wheat straw, soaked hay, supplements twice a day for her joints, magnetic tendon boots, rugs for every occasion – and that's for starters."

"Small price to pay for such a brilliant pony though?"

"Mm," Joe said, without meeting his eye.

"Problems?" Chris asked, picking up Fortune's other hind leg.

It was easier to talk when Chris was working, somehow. "She's much harder to ride than I thought she'd be," Joe admitted. "And she's so aloof. I'd give anything to be able to click with her like Harry did."

Chris lowered Fortune's leg to the floor and picked up the horseshoes he'd removed. "Sometimes horses take ages to settle into a new home," he said. "Give her time." He held her shoes up. "These are nearly worn out, so she'll need a new set. Do you want to keep them or shall I take them away?"

There was something about horseshoes; they all told a story; it was almost as if they held the spirit of the horse they'd belonged to. These were particularly special because they'd been Fortune's when she'd won the Prince Philip Cup. "I'll keep them," Joe said, taking the set of shoes from Chris and stepping aside so he could go outside to the mobile forge. There was a low whooshing noise as it was turned on.

Chris strode past him again and started to trim one of Fortune's feet.

Rusty stood waiting, his eyes fixed on the farrier, and retrieved a curled hoof clipping as soon as it fell to the ground. He carried his prize away to gnaw it in private.

Chris picked a rasp from his toolbox. "Having a good half term? What have you been up to?"

"Nothing much." Joe paused. "Actually, it has been pretty good. There was the pub quiz in The Ewe and Lamb on Friday, then aikido on Saturday. Oh, and on Sunday I went to that ploughing championship with Martin and his dad. The carthorses were awesome!"

"Didn't realise you were into heavies," Chris said.

"I'm not – I mean I wasn't. But I am now – at least, I'd love to be if I could find someone to teach me."

"Hm, there aren't many people left who know

about carthorses. I only go to one place with working Shires nowadays." There was a long pause as Chris went to get the hot shoe from the furnace so he could test whether it would be a good fit. As he offered it up to Fortune's foot, clouds of smoke rose into the air and there was an unmistakable smell. Chris studied the hoof closely, let go of the pony's leg, altered the shape of the shoe on his anvil, checked the fit again and then said, "Magnificent animals. Real gentle giants. Come along next time I go, if you like."

"That'd be great, thanks," Joe replied.

"Okay. I'll let you know." Chris began to nail the shoe in place.

Emily eventually returned with some tea. "Mum's back," she said. "She'll be out in a minute when she's put the shopping away, so you can come for a ride, Joe."

"I'm just finishing off here," Chris said, giving Fortune's hooves a final going over.

"Brill, let's tack up, then." Emily paused to make a fuss of Rusty, who knew exactly what the words *tack up* meant. "Don't worry, you can come too, you great big softie."

Joe collected Fortune's saddle and bridle from the tack room, and placed them over her stable door. As he entered, the pony shifted away from him so that her head faced the far corner.

Joe's heart sank. At HOYS she'd always greeted Harry as if he was her best friend. But Harry had grown out of Fortune, and the photos of her on his Facebook page had been replaced with photos of a big bay eventer called Barnaby, who was "a horse in a million". Harry had moved on, it seemed, even if she hadn't. Joe sighed.

Fortune looked at him momentarily before turning away again.

Tyler's attitude was easier to cope with than this; at least his apparent hatred of humans was indiscriminate. Fortune's rejection of Joe was personal. The message was polite but clear: she didn't want to be with him.

Giving her a wide berth in case she swung round suddenly, Joe approached her again and put his hand on her shoulder. Her skin shivered briefly but she didn't move. "This is hard for both of us, but let's try our best to make it work. Okay?" he said quietly. He rubbed the base of her neck, and she began to relax.

In the background he could hear Emily chattering to Chris while he rasped ET's hooves. She was talking about ET's foal, and how the vet had said it would be born towards the end of February because the gestation period for horses was eleven months – a separate conversation . . . unconnected . . . distant . . .

Fortune bent her neck round and brushed Joe's arm with her muzzle. He stroked her forehead gently. "There's a good girl," he murmured. They had a long way to go, but with any luck this was a start.

Chapter 3

They met Caroline coming out of the entrance to Lucketts Farm. "Hi there!" she said, giving Joe an irresistible smile. "Feel like some jumping? Chris has made some fences out of branches and things along the track through Parsonage Wood. Minstrel and I tried them out yesterday – they're brilliant fun!"

"Hurray, let's go!" Emily cried and stood in her stirrups, pretending to be a jockey.

Lightning trotted off with Minstrel in hot pursuit. The two girls giggled and urged their ponies on. Before long they'd turned off the road and out of sight.

Worried that her companions were abandoning

her, Fortune skittered crab-like up the road after them, her newly shod hooves striking the tarmac erratically.

Joe reined her in and felt her bunch underneath him. He tried to sit deep in the saddle, but that only made her more bouncy, like a coiled spring.

He reached the open gate the girls had gone through. It led to a field of stubble that hadn't been ploughed yet, and to his dismay he saw them breaking into a canter some distance ahead. Fortune veered through the gate, fighting for her head. Joe was about to let her go, hoping a flat-out gallop would take the wind out of her sails, when she squealed and propelled herself into the air, body hunched and all four feet off the ground, grunting with the effort.

Shock waves whipped up Joe's spine and made his shoulders ache, but he stayed on. "Hey! Caroline, Emily, wait!" he shouted.

Luckily Caroline heard him and slowed to a walk within a few strides. Emily followed, and they rode back towards him.

"Are you okay?" Caroline called.

"Yes, fine. She was being a bit of a handful, that's all," Joe said, trying to sound light-hearted even though he was rattled. "Did you see her buck?"

"No! She didn't, did she?" Emily exclaimed, her eyes wide with disbelief. "You naughty pony, Fortune!"

"She really meant it – no half measures. I don't

expect I helped much by holding her back, but I thought she'd explode if I let her go."

Caroline looked worried. "Wow, I'm really sorry. We didn't think. Do you want to carry on? We can go home now if you like."

"No, I'm sure she'll be fine as long as she doesn't get left behind again," Joe said, feeling anything but sure.

"Okay, let's ride together in a line, like the Three Musketeers," Caroline suggested. "That way we can keep an eye on each other."

"All for one and one for all!" Emily yelled, and set off at a trot.

Fortune started to canter on the spot.

"Hey, just cool it, Emily, can't you?" Joe shouted.

Emily gave him a surprised look and slowed down.

It was unusual for Joe to be the one who held everyone back. In the past he'd always been up for a race and some fooling around, confident that he'd be able to control Lightning. He'd been the impatient one when Emily was learning to ride, but now the tables had turned. Joe looked at his old pony, happily walking along with reins hanging like washing lines on each side of her neck while his little sister removed her coat, shook it out and tied it around her waist without a second thought. I hope you appreciate what a wonderful pony you've got there, Emily, he thought. I'm afraid I didn't – not really.

They walked and trotted most of the way, with a couple of short uphill canters. Fortune began to relax, and Joe did too. There was an almost ethereal lightness to her; her paces were so floating that Joe could hardly tell whether her feet were touching the ground.

By the time they reached Parsonage Wood he was feeling pretty confident. Although he hadn't done much jumping because he'd been so focused on mounted games, he'd always enjoyed it. Fortune would know what she was doing, anyway. He'd seen photos of her leaping over some horrendous obstacles, and Harry had mentioned she'd been a show jumper before she became a games pony. That small bundle of branches on the grass in front of them actually looked rather inviting.

"The rest of them are in the wood; Chris made this as a sort of practice fence," Caroline said. "Who's going first?"

"I will, if you like," Joe said with a rush of nervous excitement. He wanted to prove he wasn't a wimp – to himself as well as the girls.

Fortune went up a gear as soon as she realised she was going to be asked to jump. Her elastic energy felt thrilling and slightly scary.

Joe cantered in a large circle to settle her, trying to

remember all the things he'd been taught: straight approach, positive attitude, gentle hands and count the final three strides before take-off . . . As he guided her out of the circle, her stride lengthened and they accelerated towards the fence as if it was pulling them in like a magnet . . . One, two . . . Fortune launched herself into the air before Joe had a chance to count the third stride. Luckily he was already leaning forward in jumping position, so he just about stayed with her. She landed and bowled on, ears pricked, looking for the next one. Reluctantly, Joe slowed her down and returned to the girls.

"Wow! That looked *amazing*!" Caroline said.

He couldn't stop grinning. "Your turn," he said, stroking Fortune's warm neck.

They each jumped the fence twice without any problems, so they decided to move on to the jumps in the wood.

"You lead, then Fortune won't get worried about being left behind." Caroline said to Joe.

"Yup, good idea. I haven't a clue where I'm going, though."

"Don't worry, follow your nose."

"Okay. Come on, Fortune, let's party!" Joe said, and headed into the unknown.

The first obstacle caught him unawares because his eyes were still adjusting to the shade, but Fortune negotiated it without a hitch. He was ready for the second one, though, and got the timing exactly right. They sailed over. It felt so perfect that he welled up inside with emotion. All the doubts he'd had about whether she was the right pony for him melted away as she powered along with a steady, eager rhythm. Another jump came and went, and he let out a whoop of pure joy.

He didn't want this to end . . . but it did, and sooner than expected.

By the time Joe saw the pheasants on the track it was too late. They stayed put until Fortune was nearly on top of them and then rose with a flurry of whirring wings, calling shrilly. The air filled with feathers and noise. Fortune swerved and bolted. *Thump!* A pheasant hit Joe's shoulder. He swayed off balance and found himself lying halfway up his pony's neck, hanging on somehow. Wind whistled past his ears and blurred his vision as he struggled to sit upright and gain control. Inevitably, another jump appeared. Fortune hardly saw it in her panic and Joe was in no position to help her. She ploughed through, stumbling over the tangled branches. Sensing she'd lost momentum, he made a huge effort and heaved himself back into the saddle – just in time to see a solid tree trunk approaching. He managed to gather up the reins as Fortune started to accelerate again.

"Steady! Steady!" he said breathlessly, and felt her checking, but the jump was coming up fast so he decided to let her go for it after all. Sensing his hesitation, Fortune slid to a standstill. Joe catapulted over her head. His thigh bashed against the log before he slid into some churned-up mud on the far side. He instinctively huddled into a ball, waiting for the others to jump, but the hoof beats slowed and he could hear the girls talking.

"Where is he?"

"Oh, look!"

Emily giggled. "What are you doing down there? You do look funny, Joe! You're covered with mud!"

Joe uncurled himself, still rather dazed. "Pheasants startled her. I fell off."

"Are you okay?" Caroline asked.

He clambered to his feet gingerly. His leg hurt.

"Lucky you had a nice soft landing," Emily said, grinning at the sight of him.

"Yes," Caroline added. "No harm done."

Joe smiled weakly. The landing hadn't been nice *or* soft and he was pretty sure harm *had* been done. Fortune had put her trust in him and something scary had happened which had shaken both of them. He had an awful feeling she might never trust him again.

Chapter 4

On the last Saturday of half term, Nellie came over to help Joe get the horses stabled for the night while Mum took Emily to a friend's birthday party in Bellsham Leisure Centre.

When they went into the Long Meadow, Fortune walked up to Nellie rather than Joe. He tried not to mind, and picked up Lightning's head collar instead.

"What do you feel about Fortune?" Nellie asked while Joe was catching Lightning – or, to be more accurate, Lightning was catching him. She always came up and put her nose straight into her head collar.

Joe hesitated. A single word came into his head immediately, but he was reluctant to say it. "Honestly?"

"Yes, honestly."

"Disappointment," he said, and instantly realised how bad that sounded. "Not just with her. I'm disappointed in myself too," he added. "I get the feeling that Fortune realises I'm not good enough for her. She's a brilliant pony – everyone knows that – so it must be me. You know you told me that every time a person rides a horse they're training it, even if they're just going out for a hack? Well, I'm becoming afraid to do anything because I seem to be making her worse all the time and I don't know how to put it right." He looked fondly at his old pony and sighed. "I thought Fortune was going to be perfect, my dream pony, like a larger version of Lightning only even better, but she's completely different."

"Perhaps Fortune thought you'd be a smaller version of Harry," Nellie said.

"Hm, I don't think she's that stupid." Joe paused. "Oh, I see what you mean!"

Nellie smiled. "Horses are excellent mirrors. They reflect our feelings."

Joe instantly felt guilty. "I've blown it, haven't I?" he said miserably. "I've ruined her."

"Don't talk rubbish," Nellie replied. "You just need to go back to basics, that's all."

"You mean do lots of walking before I start trotting, like I did with Lightning?" Joe asked.

"Even more basic than that. Go into her field and observe her. Get to know what she's like with other horses. Let her become used to you being around. Spend as much time as possible together." Nellie smiled. "When I was younger, travelling around the countryside with my family, we lived with our horses and got to know them really well – almost as if we were all part of the same herd. It's a pity so few people can experience that nowadays." A dreamy look came over her for a moment before her attention switched to Joe again. "Yes, try to spend a whole day with Fortune, doing nothing in particular. You'll be astonished how much you learn about each other."

The following evening, after supper, Joe took a torch and walked up the road to Orchard Rise with Rusty. He wanted to tell Nellie what he'd found out.

Her face lit up as she opened her front door. "Come in! Hot chocolate?"

"Yes, please," Joe replied. Nellie made the best hot chocolate ever. He sat down on the comfy old sofa while she clattered around in her overcrowded kitchen. She didn't believe in instant food, and made everything from raw ingredients. Her hot chocolate was real chocolate grated into hot milk, with a sprinkle of cinnamon on top.

Rusty lay down in front of the wood burner with a contented sigh, and Mittens the cat jumped off Nellie's armchair to snuggle up beside him. Rusty seemed to get on with every kind of animal, and politely made himself at home wherever he happened to be.

Joe felt at home in Orchard Rise too. It was cosy and cluttered, with a fascinating assortment of ornaments jostling for position on every available surface.

Nellie emerged from the kitchen carrying two china mugs decorated with pictures of horses and wagons. She handed one to Joe and sat down in her armchair. They sipped their drinks, watching flames licking against the glass of the wood burner.

"I don't know why I ever thought Lightning and Fortune were alike," Joe said after a while. "They're completely different, aren't they?"

Nellie turned to look at him, and smiled.

"I couldn't spend the whole day with her because I had homework to do – we're back to school tomorrow – but even so I found out a lot just being in the field for a couple of hours." Joe took another gulp of hot chocolate. "Lightning keeps out of trouble and does her own thing, but all the other horses seem to love her and follow her around. It's sort of like she's the boss, although she's not at all bossy. I suppose they follow her around because they trust her."

"And Fortune?" Nellie asked.

"She's jealous of any horse that gets too near Lightning, and the others keep out of her way. She's like a new girl at school who's latched onto somebody, desperate to be their best friend."

"How did they react to you being in the field with them?"

Joe gave a short laugh. "To begin with Lady wouldn't leave me alone, but she eventually lost interest when she decided I didn't have any food. Lightning came to say hello every now and then. I stroked her and we had a good chat, and then she wandered off again. She didn't seem at all surprised that I was there."

"What about Fortune?"

"She tagged along with Lightning, but she was always a few steps behind. She seemed suspicious of me. I think she wondered what I wanted, so I told her I wanted to get to know her and be her friend," Joe said. He'd have felt foolish saying that to anyone but Nellie.

"Good for you."

"And it seemed to work." This was the bit he'd been longing to tell her. "Because she came right up to me after that. I gave her a good rub underneath her mane, and her bottom lip went all quivery."

Nellie chuckled.

"So we stood together for quite a while," Joe went on, "and I thought about all sorts of things, like how lost I felt when we moved here from Birmingham. I mean, at least I knew what was going on, even if I wished it hadn't happened, but she must have been so bewildered when she arrived here." He paused to drink from his mug. "I also remembered riding her back from the early morning practice session at the Horse of the Year Show with Harry, and how impressed I was that I could control her just by thinking what I wanted to do. Then I remembered how it felt when we were jumping together, before we bumped into those pheasants, and that was when she bent her neck round and touched me really softly with her muzzle. It happened once before, when I was talking to her in her stable, so I don't think it was a fluke."

"I'm sure it wasn't. Time well spent, then. Was it fun jumping with her?"

"Amazing!" Joe said, alive with the memory of it. "For a while I forgot to be worried that other people were watching. In fact, I wasn't really thinking of anything at all, just feeling."

"Living in the moment," Nellie said.

"Yes, exactly."

She looked pleased. "Horses live in the moment, and the way to connect with them is to be there too. It doesn't help at all if you're worrying about what other people think or whether someone else is better than you."

Harry, Joe thought fleetingly. "The thing is," he said, "I know what I saw today, and it was really interesting, but I'm not sure how I should make use of it."

"Good point," Nellie replied. "Well, would you describe Lightning as a leader or a follower?"

She had a habit of answering one question with another. Joe had found it disconcerting at first, but he was beginning to understand why she did it. Working out the answer for himself meant much more than being told.

"She's a leader," he said. "All the other horses rely on her to look after them. I'm starting to realise how much she looked after me as well."

"Yes, she's a very special pony, that one," Nellie said. "What about Fortune?"

"Definitely a follower. She's quite insecure, isn't she?"

"Sensitive animals often are, especially where humans are concerned. She'll pick up on your emotions and react to them just like that." Nellie clicked her fingers as she said it. "If you're nervous, she'll be nervous. However, if you keep calm and prove you're a dependable leader she'll follow you to the ends of the earth. Gain her trust and she'll give you everything she's got." She offered Joe a homemade biscuit and took one herself. "You were right all along, you know. Fortune *is* the perfect pony for you. Some people spend a lifetime around horses without understanding them properly – they don't learn that good horsemanship is more about feel than techniques, so they never make much progress." A grin spread over her face. "You will, though. She'll teach you more than you ever dreamed possible."

Chapter 5

They had many more enquiries about places at the Hidden Horseshoe as the days became shorter and grassy fields were trampled to a muddy pulp. Mum took in a few of the most desperate cases, but there really wasn't much room left. Even with Nellie and Debbie helping it was a struggle to get all the work done.

Joe, too, found that looking after a pony wasn't easy in the winter, especially when he had to juggle it with school. From Monday to Friday he caught the bus just as it was getting light, and by the time he got home again it was dark.

He soon gave up any idea of riding Fortune on weekdays. Instead, he went to her stable and spent time with her. Sometimes he took his sketchbook, sat on an upturned bucket and drew her for his art project at school. He studied her in detail from every angle: her deep, almond-shaped eyes with grey lashes, the grey dapples over her body, her two-tone tail with light hairs on the top and darker ones underneath, the delicate curve of her neck and the slope of her shoulder. She really was an incredible creature. How did those slim legs manage to gallop, turn and jump so effortlessly? In fact, how did she carry him, especially when the saddle was clamped over her rib cage where she had no legs to support the extra weight? Extraordinary – he'd never really thought about it before. He found himself saying things like, "What a beautiful girl you are," and then checking anxiously to make sure nobody was nearby. If Emily heard him talking to his pony like that she was bound to tease him about it, even though she was always calling Lightning things like "Sweetie-pie".

Even though Joe wasn't riding Fortune much, he made sure he groomed her regularly. After a while he just used his hands because she seemed to prefer it – and having brushed the back of his hand with a dandy brush to see what it felt like, he understood why. He could be much more gentle and adapt to the angles and curves of her body with his hands. In a way it was more like massaging than grooming.

Soon Fortune was greeting Joe with an affectionate whinny, and she wanted to be with him so much that it was difficult to get her to stand back while he drew her. She had a habit of taking a mouthful of hay and dunking it in her water bucket, and she ruined several sketches by nudging his hand and slobbering over the paper. At least, he thought she'd ruined them, but his art teacher thought they were "marvellously organic", so that was okay.

Opportunities to ride were confined to weekends, and, even then, Saturday afternoons were ruled out because of aikido. Joe, Martin and Caroline were in the same group, and they usually spent time in town together afterwards.

The lessons were always a highlight of Joe's week. It wasn't so much the actual aikido, although that was fun, but the way that Sensei Radford, their teacher, taught them to see life from a different perspective. He'd encouraged Joe to think about lots of things, and what he'd learned had helped him in all sorts of ways – especially where horses and riding were concerned. The subject of the last lesson before the Christmas holidays struck a particular chord with Joe.

"Water is a central theme of Japanese philosophy and literature," Sensei Radford said. "The Japanese are acutely aware of the power of water. It is a vital element that can both nurture life and cause death and destruction." His eyes scanned his students. "Martin. Can you tell us anything else about water?"

"It's wet," said Martin, and the class giggled. "But fish seem to like it."

Sensei Radford's deadpan face put an end to any more noise. "So, tell me about the lake where you go fishing. What does the surface look like on a completely calm day?"

"Kind of glassy – clear and still."

"Good. And when you throw a stone into the lake? What happens then?"

"Other fishermen get cross," Martin said, and put a hand to his mouth as everyone started laughing again. "Oh, what happens to the *water*? Er, ripples travel from the centre and mess up the clear surface?"

"Very good. Thank you, Martin," Sensei Radford said. "Does anyone know what *Mizu no kokoro* means?" They looked blank, so told he told them. "It means 'a mind like water'. It's important, though, to remember that *kokoro* in Japanese means the heart *and* mind together. Emotions and rational thought are often separated in Western culture, but the Japanese believe they are intertwined." He paused.

"So, why is it a good thing to have a mind like water? Think of that calm fishing lake. The surface is still and the water takes on a mirror-like quality, reflecting how things are in reality. In this state your mind can think clearly, without emotion. This means you can keep calm in adversity, which can be very useful."

Joe remembered Nellie saying something similar after Mum had fallen off Lady, but she'd been talking about horses keeping calm and in balance then.

"*However*, I'm not saying you should accept whatever life throws at you," Sensei Radford continued. "Think of the ripples that form on the surface of that lake when Martin throws a stone into it. Would the size of his stone make a difference to the size of the ripples?"

They all nodded.

"Yes, the reaction of water to any disturbance is always in perfect harmony with it – neither more nor less than is appropriate. Water never overreacts, but it never underreacts either, and it soon returns to its original calmness. That is how you should be, in aikido and in life." Sensei Radford smiled. "Easier said than done, I know. How do we gauge what level of reaction is appropriate? Consider those angry fishermen on the bank. Martin has frightened away the fish and disturbed a peaceful afternoon by throwing a stone into the water. Should they do nothing, politely ask him not to throw any more stones or throw him into the lake?"

"Throw him in," Darren and Spike mumbled simultaneously, and the rest of them couldn't help laughing.

Sensei Radford raised his hands for silence. "Mm, I can see your point, but the middle way is probably the one I should advocate," he said. "So, to summarise: strive to develop a mind that – like water – is naturally balanced and calm, but don't be completely submissive. Adapt to whatever life gives you and try to harmonise with it. React appropriately, from your inner self, to events in your life. *Osu.*"

Joe had the chance to put this advice to the test the following week. It was the first day of the Christmas holidays, and unusually warm and dry for the time of year. He got up as soon as it was light because he wanted to ride Fortune early so she'd be able to relax in the field for the rest of the day.

It was the Bellsham Vale Pony Club Christmas rally in four days' time, and the party traditionally ended with some team gymkhana games. It wasn't meant to be a serious rally but Joe knew all eyes would be on Fortune, the champion games pony, and that the selectors for next year's mounted games teams would be especially interested. He was keen to get her going as well as possible in the limited time available.

Emily was still in her dressing gown – it always took her ages to get going in the mornings – so Joe decided to go out on a hack by himself. Perhaps they'd be able to practise a few mounted games techniques together later on.

Fortune hadn't been ridden for several days. She jigged and sidestepped, spooking at everything from the wheelie bin outside the front gate to a drainage grille in the road that she'd never noticed before. She even pretended to be scared of Rusty, who was padding along behind as usual.

Joe became vigilant, scanning the road ahead for potential problems, especially as they approached the bridge at the bottom of the hill. She'd taken a dislike to it, probably because her hooves made a hollow echo and the river was clearly visible on each side. Cars made an odd noise too – something to do with the way it had been built out of concrete and metal.

Fortune stiffened, arched her neck and slowed down when they arrived at the bridge. Her ears pricked so they were nearly touching, and she snorted suspiciously.

Any moment now she's going to wheel round and head for home, Joe thought. He shortened the reins and drove her on with his seat and legs. She ground to a halt. Remembering his aikido lesson, Joe tried to visualise a tranquil lake, although he didn't really expect it to help much. Fortune calmed down almost instantly. Had their minds become connected in some way, or was it just that he'd relaxed more? Whatever the reason, it worked. She walked over the bridge and settled into a buoyant trot up the road.

Joe heard a lorry rumbling over the bridge and changing gear for the hill. Fortune was almost opposite the gate of the bridlepath to Lucketts Farm, so he decided to cross the road and quickly undo the latch of the gate.

Rusty dashed through as he started to open it . . . *Kok kok kok kok kok!* A couple of pheasants whizzed by. Joe felt the agitation of the pheasants, the heavy vibrations of the approaching lorry and Fortune's quivering uncertainty, yet he calmly urged her forwards through the gate, out of harm's way. She obeyed without question.

It was only when the danger had passed and they were standing safely in the field that Joe realised his heart was thumping. He dismounted, landing on wobbly legs, and made a fuss of his pony. As they stood there another pheasant flew out of the hedge, wings whirring, but Fortune hardly noticed it; all her attention was on Joe. He praised her some more and then vaulted on and headed for home with a jubilant feeling that something important had happened.

He'd earned her trust.

Chapter 6

A week later, just before Christmas, Joe had a phone call from Chris.

"You doing anything?" he asked.

"Don't think so, apart from the usual – horses and stuff. Why?" Joe replied.

"I'm going to shoe those Shires I was telling you about. Want to come along?"

"Oh!" Joe had almost given up hoping that Chris would remember the offer he'd made nearly two months ago.

"Sorry it's rather last minute."

"That's okay," Joe said. "I'd love to come, thanks." There was no way he was going to miss the chance of seeing some Shire horses!

"Great. I'll pick you up in half an hour."

"Sure you've got everything?" Chris said with amusement as Joe struggled into the front seat of the van with his wellies, waterproofs and a carrier bag containing gloves, a woolly hat and a packed lunch complete with a flask of tomato soup.

"Sorry, had to bring it all to keep Mum happy," Joe said, shoving his belongings into the space on the floor around his feet. There was no room anywhere else. The back of the van held all the tools of Chris' trade and the compartments at the front were filled with an intriguing mixture of CDs, invoice books, pens, horseshoe nails and studs, coins, some pincers, a riding hat, windscreen de-icer and other bits and bobs. Joe loved everything about the white van, right down to its noisy industrial-strength heater and ripped, dog-hairy seat covers; just travelling in it made him feel workman-like.

Chris' driving style was the same as his riding. He appeared to be totally relaxed and yet had razor-sharp reactions when necessary. "I hear you and Fortune swept the board at the Pony Club Christmas rally yesterday," he commented after a while.

"Who told you that?" Joe asked, pleased.

"Caroline and Tracey couldn't stop talking about it. Caroline's getting excited about the Bellsham Vale's chances of winning the Prince Philip Cup this year. She's already got the mounted games team worked out: you on Fortune, Emily on Lightning, her on Minstrel, Ali on Rolo and Sarah on Flicka."

Joe smiled. He'd been thinking along the same lines last night in bed as he'd replayed the events of the afternoon over in his head, too elated to go to sleep. "Yup, we'd make a pretty good team, I reckon," he replied.

Fortune had been het up at the start of the rally – it hadn't helped that everyone had been in Christmassy fancy dress – but Joe had thought of the calm lake again, which had helped a lot, and she'd soon settled once she'd realised she had a job to do.

He'd always thought that Lightning was fast, but Fortune was like a jet-propelled rocket! It had taken him completely by surprise in the first race, and he'd nearly fallen off backwards. Also, he'd soon discovered that Fortune needed much more guidance. Lightning, he realised now, had looked after him and shown him what to do. Fortune, on the other hand, needed instructions all the way. The good news, though, was that she did whatever was asked of her instantly, without question, and she was so sensitive that Joe only had to think something and she did it.

"I'm glad you're getting on with Fortune. Always takes time adjusting to a new horse," Chris said.

"Yup, I realise that now. She's so different from Lightning," Joe said. "They're rather like two settings on a camera. Lightning's autofocus – you always get a good result with her unless you do something really stupid. But Fortune's definitely an advanced manual setting – you have to know what you're doing, and it takes a lot of fine tuning, but if you get it right the results are amazing."

Chris chuckled. "What's Lady, then? Wide angle?"

Joe grinned. "Definitely. And ET's zoom!"

They both laughed, then fell into a companionable silence again.

Joe looked out of the window. As far as he was concerned they were travelling in uncharted territory – farmland interrupted at regular intervals by houses. Some had stables attached, and the fields often had post-and-rail fencing and jumps of various shapes and sizes.

As usual, Joe wondered about each horse or pony he saw. What did those expensive-looking horses wearing lots of rugs do? There were some enormous jumps a couple of fields away, so perhaps they were racehorses or eventers . . . Unusual to see so many small ponies in one field. He guessed they were Shetlands . . . Was that hairy coloured cob used for riding or driving? It looked rather like Lady, but even muddier. Not surprising, considering the state of its field . . .

Disford Welcomes Careful Drivers, a road sign announced. Chris reduced his speed to what seemed like a crawl and steered the van through a narrow street with buildings on either side. They passed a pub called The Plough. Its eye-catching sign was of two Shire horses ploughing under a fiery sky.

An ancient-looking church came into view, and then the van turned down a lane signposted *Church Farm*, through a gate and into a cobbled courtyard surrounded by stone buildings that looked every bit as old as the church.

How strange to have a farm right in the middle of a village, Joe thought as he and Chris got out of the van. He felt as if he'd been transported a hundred years back in time. Nothing he could see, apart from the white van, gave any indication of the modern world. Some chickens and a couple of ducks wandered about and rootled around in the muckheap, and two huge horses – one black and one dappled grey – stood tied to a wall, their rounded rumps tilted towards each other as they each rested a hind leg. Their shaggy winter coats hadn't been clipped but there wasn't a speck of mud on either of them.

They're just like smaller versions of Velvet and Sherman, Joe thought.

As if to complete the picture, a man appeared wearing work boots, thick brown trousers and a tweed coat and hat. He stood leaning on a thumb-stick for a moment, looking at his visitors through round-rimmed spectacles.

Joe recognised him instantly. Oh my goodness, he thought, hardly daring to believe it was true. Those horses *are* Velvet and Sherman!

"Morning," the man said. He came over and held out his hand to Chris, then Joe. "I'm Malc. Are you Chris' apprentice?"

Joe felt relieved that Malc hadn't recognised him as the boy who'd stood gawping at the ploughing match. "Um, no," he said. "Wish I was, but I haven't finished school yet."

"Joe often comes with me in the holidays," Chris explained. "And I thought he'd enjoy today, knowing how interested he is in heavy horses."

Malc smiled. "Well in that case you'd better come and meet my two."

Joe followed him.

Malc went to the shoulder of the black horse first. "This is Velvet. She's fourteen years old, and I bred her myself. Owned her mother and her grand-mother before that. Excellent plough horse. Right temperament, see? Good and steady, with a handy stubborn streak that means she doesn't give up on a job in a hurry." He gave Velvet's thick, hairy neck a pat.

She turned her head as far as her lead rope would allow, and nuzzled him in return.

"And this handsome chap's Sherman," he said, ducking under the mare's head. "Velvet bred four foals, and he was the last and the best."

Such huge, solid creatures should have been intimidating but Joe felt completely at home. They had a peacefulness about them that Nellie would have called "good energy".

He stroked the dense teddy-bear fur on Sherman's dappled neck. "They look wonderful."

"My pride and joy," Malc said, looking pleased.

Chris came up to Velvet and ran his hand down her foreleg. She lifted her hoof instantly, and with a few deft movements he began removing her shoe.

Joe stood watching. There wasn't much he could do to help, but he liked collecting the shoes so he could take the old nails out and put them safely in a box. He took the shoe from Chris, and studied the chunky arc of metal in his hands. Apart from its size, it was different from the shoes Chris normally used. To keep costs down, he usually bought in factory-made shoes of various sizes which had nail holes punched at regular intervals, and he then adapted them to fit individual horses, but this had seven rectangular holes – four on the outside and three on the inside – with a nail sticking out of each one. "Is this hand-made?" he asked.

"Yes, only the best for Malc," Chris said, handing Joe another.

"Mass-produced ones are a false economy," Malc said. "You can't beat a properly made shoe."

When Chris had removed all four he straightened his back. "Refits all round, I reckon."

Joe went to the van, put the old nails away safely and placed the shoes by the portable forge in the back of the van. Then he collected Sherman's shoes and did the same with them. After that he made himself useful wherever he could: fetching things for Chris or sweeping up nail fragments and dung. When there didn't seem to be anything else to do, he stood by the horses and watched Chris work. He never tired of that.

The horses behaved impeccably. Despite their size, they lifted their legs on cue and balanced themselves like equine ballerinas while Chris worked.

Joe watched as Chris held one of Sherman's shoes in place and started to nail it onto the base of his foot. "Is that much more difficult than normal?" he asked once the rhythmical hammering had petered out.

"No, easier – especially as they're so well-mannered," Chris replied. "Their hooves have nice thick walls and it's not so far for me to bend over." He glanced up at Joe. "I'd rather shoe a Shire than a Shetland any day." He took another nail from his toolbox, and the chime of his hammer filled the stone courtyard again.

When Chris had just about finished, Malc said, "How about giving them an airing?"

Chris put down the file he'd been using and lifted Velvet's colossal hoof off the tripod so she could stand on all four legs again, then he stretched. "Have you got time, Joe?" he asked. "You don't have to get back for anything, do you?"

"Yes, I don't think so, I mean no." Joe took a deep breath, so excited he couldn't think straight, and tried again. "No, I don't think I've got to get back for anything, and yes, I'd love to go out for a drive with the horses – please. I mean thank you."

Malc's face creased into a smile. "Well then, boys. We'd better get some harness."

Chapter 7

The walls of the shed were festooned with an orderly yet bewildering array of leather and metal – some shiny, some plain and worn, but all of it spotless.

Joe looked around in awe, breathing in the intoxicating smell of clean leather. He recognised a dazzling set of brown harness with brass fittings hanging on the far wall. Sherman and Velvet had worn it at the ploughing match.

Malc reached for a couple of black leather-backed collars hanging on the wall. "I'll take these and some collar pads if you boys bring the rest. We'll use the American pairs harness. Bring out Velvet's first, could you?"

Joe followed Chris over to a spaghetti-like mass of black leather draped between two large hooks hanging from the ceiling.

"Okay," Chris said. "If you hold the back end of the harness, I'll grab the hames and we'll sling it on as one."

Joe struggled out of the door, trying not to trip over the dangling straps as he followed Chris across the yard.

"When I lift the hames over Velvet's collar, you sling your bit over her backside, so the traces in your right hand end up on the other side," Chris said, handling his part with ease.

Joe worked out that the traces were the two longest, thickest strips of leather. He lugged the mass of harness up and over Velvet's ample bottom, being careful not to alarm her. She stood still, as solid as a rock.

The hames fitted snugly into the groove in Velvet's collar. Malc buckled them together with a strap underneath, and then worked his way over the harness – explaining which pieces buckled or clipped to others as he went. Joe tried to concentrate and remember it all, but it seemed incredibly complicated.

Chris collected the other set of harness by himself, in a neat bundle with the hames over his shoulder. He walked up to Sherman and tossed the whole thing on in one go.

Malc fetched a couple of bridles. "Always put these on last and take them off first," he said. "Once horses have their blinkers on they can't see what's going on around them." He eased Velvet's bridle over her head and clipped the outside rein onto the bit. "A lot of heavy horse people use these Liverpool bits. Velvet can be quite strong sometimes, so I'm putting her reins one notch below the ring for more control, but Sherman's will be on the ring because he hardly needs a bit at all. He can be driven by voice alone most of the time."

Malc put Sherman's bridle on as well. Then he crossed over the horses' inside reins. "Do you see how this works, Joe?" he asked. "Further back, here, the reins split into two so that the long rein the driver holds in his right hand connects to the horses' off-side bits and the one he holds in his left hand goes to their near-sides. One pair of reins to control two horses – clever, eh?"

Joe tried to work it out, but his brain had information overload. He hadn't realised that driving heavy horses would be so different from riding ponies. Now that Velvet and Sherman were harnessed and alert they looked even larger – as he remembered them at the ploughing match, in fact.

"Is the hitch cart in the shed?" Chris asked.

"Yes, if you two get it out I'll drive the horses over."

The cart didn't look like a proper old-fashioned cart at all – more like a bench on wheels, with a painted frame made from angle iron and a metal pole sticking out at the front with a T-piece on the end. *Clunk!* It settled onto the cobbles, and Chris told Joe to stand back.

To Joe's amazement, Malc drove the horses towards the highest part of the pole, at a sharp angle. Sherman was the first to reach it; he stepped over nimbly, turned to the front and stood still. Velvet turned at the same time so they were standing side by side with the pole between them.

How cool is that? Joe thought.

Chris helped to lift the pole so that the straps hanging from the hames could be clipped onto each side of the T-piece. "You always do this before clipping the traces to the whipple trees," he said.

Joe watched carefully as Chris attached the traces, and worked out that the whipple trees were hinged horizontal bars. He'd never remember all this!

Malc heaved himself up onto the cart, and Joe and Chris climbed on board as well so that all three of them were on the long, padded seat.

Joe was no longer a mere spectator; he was sitting in the driving seat! Two Shire horses stood hitched before him, ready for work. The moment he'd longed for was actually happening.

"Here you are, son," Malc said, handing Joe the reins. "The best way to learn is to do it."

They were much thicker than normal reins, and their immense length weighed heavily so it was difficult for Joe to gauge what sort of contact he had with the horses' mouths. "How do I hold them?" he asked.

"Some folk hold them like you would for riding, and some just run them up through their hands. Whatever suits, really," Malc said.

The rules seem wonderfully flexible compared with riding, Joe thought. In the Pony Club there are definite right and wrong ways to do pretty well everything. "How do I make them go?" he asked.

"Up to you. I use a kissing noise, but if you'd rather not then just ask them to walk on."

The horses stood with relaxed necks and floppy ears. They looked as if they'd gone to sleep. If Joe had been riding them he'd have squeezed with his legs – or possibly even given a little kick to wake them up – but they were way out in front of him and his only physical connection with them was through the reins. In westerns, waggoners often whacked the horses with their reins, cracked whips and shouted things like "Yee-ha!" Joe realised that was a bit extreme, but flicking the horses seemed a good idea. "Walk on!" he ordered, and at the same time shook the heavy reins. They slapped against the horses' rumps with much more force than he'd intended.

The result was immediate and dramatic. They plunged forwards, starting the cart with a tremendous jolt that nearly threw him from the seat, and set off at a brisk trot.

Joe pulled back on the reins as hard as he could but they had too much slack in them, even when he leaned right back, and the horses were gaining momentum with every stride. The cart bounced over the cobbles, frustrating his efforts to regain control.

Malc grabbed the reins from Joe's hands. "Whoa there! Steady!"

The horses' ears swivelled to pick up the familiar commands, and they slowed to a walk, then a standstill.

"Sorry," Joe said breathlessly. "I don't think I'm strong enough. You'd better drive them."

"Nonsense," Malc replied. "There isn't a person alive who'd pit their strength against nearly two tonnes of Shire horse. You don't need strength, you need skill, and a good deal of that comes by learning from your mistakes." He handed the reins back to Joe. "Let's start over, shall we?"

Joe felt nervous about trying again but didn't want to say so.

"The first thing you've got to realise is these are horses, with the same sensitivities as other horses and ponies. You wouldn't slap your riding pony with those reins and expect to get away with it, would you?"

Joe shook his head.

"I've seen a lot of folk run into trouble with Shires because they take liberties with them. It's true that Velvet and Sherman are calmer than your average thoroughbred, and they're built for different work, but basically they're bigger and stronger versions of the kind of horses you're used to at home."

Joe nodded. He'd felt first-hand how powerful they could be.

"There's an art to working horses that has little to do with strength and everything to do with feel and timing," Malc went on. "When you're driving them you've got your voice, the reins and an invisible connection you can only build up if you're patient, see?"

Joe nodded again. "Yes."

"So, treat these horses with respect, as you would your riding pony. Always start your signals softly and build them up until they take notice. Be firm but fair. Leave off as soon as you get a response, and you'll find next time you can be even softer until you can almost drive them by sixth sense."

Joe smiled to himself.

"Right then," Malc said, putting his hands over Joe's to guide them. "Hold your reins so you have a light contact at all times – about there for now. If you need to shorten them, hold both in one hand while you move the other hand up. Constantly feel what's happening between you, the horses and the cart, and adjust things accordingly. Hands low, sit up straight, shoulders relaxed. The horses get a lot of information from those reins, and they'll be able to tell whether you're tense or not, see? Okay, when you're ready, politely tell them to walk on."

Joe took a deep breath and looked straight ahead, determined to get it right this time. "Walk on," he said.

And the horses walked on.

Chapter 8

It snowed on Christmas Eve and the freezing weather lasted for over a week. In a way, Joe was glad. There was something magical about a white Christmas, especially as his grandparents, aunt and young cousins were staying for a few days. They did all sorts of fun wintery things, like tobogganing and building snowmen.

Sub-zero temperatures always made looking after animals more difficult, though. Water froze in troughs and buckets, and the horses became skittish from lack of exercise. Joe was particularly concerned whenever they set ET loose in her field, remembering how she'd dashed around in the snow the year before. A fall on icy ground now that she was heavily in foal could be disastrous. But he needn't have worried; being pregnant had calmed her down, and she wandered around the field looking responsible and matronly.

Joe managed to get some great photos of Fortune and Lightning playing in the snow together while their field was still white and pristine. He posted them on Facebook, pleased to be able to show Harry how happy Fortune was and tell him what a star she'd been at the Pony Club Christmas rally. He emailed Mrs McCulloch, her owner, with similar news and some photos. She replied almost immediately, saying how glad she was that Fortune had found such a good home. Joe decided she wasn't fussy after all – just a caring owner wanting the best for her pony.

Dad's Christmas present to Mum was a double horse trailer. They'd exchanged the family car for a Land Rover some time ago, so now they'd be able to transport horses and ponies themselves.

Slowly but surely they were getting all the equipment they needed and, despite small and rather chaotic beginnings, the Hidden Horseshoe Sanctuary was becoming a successful business.

*

A major disadvantage of the snow was that it prevented Joe from going to see Sherman and Velvet again. His brief experience of driving them had made him fascinated about everything to do with working horses, and he spent hours reading about them on the internet. He discovered he wasn't alone; there were loads of heavy horse enthusiasts all over the place. There was even a magazine called *Heavy Horse World*, and he used some of his Christmas money to pay for a subscription.

Joe began to notice things to do with heavy horses wherever he went – a pair of hames and a set of whipple trees hanging on the wall in the Ewe and Lamb, for instance, or a rusty old horse plough abandoned in a hedge by Parsonage Wood. Martin said he was becoming obsessed with anything to do with horses, but Joe pointed out that he was a fine one to talk when all he thought about was fishing.

It wasn't until after the New Year, when there were only a few more days of the holidays left, that Chris managed to take the afternoon off and drive Joe to Church Farm again. The roads were clear, but snow still lay in the fields and in messy ribbons along the verges.

"I'll be glad when everything thaws properly,"

Chris said as they drove along. "Keeping the point-to-pointers fit in this weather's a nightmare."

"Yes, we've hardly ridden at all this holidays, and I was hoping to do a lot with Fortune. It's always such a rush during term time, and it won't be long before the trials for this year's mounted games team."

"You're welcome to use the indoor school at Lucketts."

"Thanks." Joe looked out of the window to spot the horses he'd noticed last time they'd made the journey. He couldn't see the classy-looking horses. They were probably in their stables . . . The Shetlands were barely visible, grazing a different field further away from the road . . . The coloured cob that looked like Lady was in its field, though. It was standing by the fence, hock-deep in mud, watching the traffic go by. Suddenly Joe wished he'd asked Chris to stop so they could check the horse was okay, but the moment had passed.

Sherman and Velvet were still outside when Chris and Joe arrived at Church Farm.

"Didn't want to spoil you too much by getting them all cleaned up and ready," Malc said.

Joe understood what he meant when he saw how muddy they were. It was hard to imagine how they'd looked at the ploughing match, with pristine coats, colourful flights in their manes – he now knew those upright ribbons were called flights – and chalky-white leg feathers.

It took a whole hour to clean Sherman and Velvet. Joe's hands were frozen because he had to hose off their legs with cold water.

"Remind me to put oil on them when we get back," Malc said as they harnessed the horses. "Can't beat pig oil and flowers of sulphur for protecting their legs in this weather."

The harness was no longer a complete mystery to Joe. He'd learned what the main parts were called and how they fitted together, and he tried his best to be useful: fetching, lifting, adjusting, buckling and clipping.

At last they were hitched up and ready to go.

Malc handed Joe the reins. "Remember what to do?"

He nodded.

"Good. When you get to the road, turn right. We'll take a different route today."

They went down the road, past the pub and the sign welcoming careful drivers to Disford. A lorry rattled by. Its tyres made a swishing noise on the wet road. Joe prepared himself for a reaction, but Velvet and Sherman didn't even flick their ears. They just kept trotting with an easy-going rhythm along the wide, meandering road away from the village.

After a while he began to relax. The snow-streaked countryside looked desolate. He shivered. You definitely get colder driving than you do when you're riding, he thought. I suppose it's because you use your body much more when you're riding. Driving's a doddle in comparison.

More cars whooshed by. Some of the passengers smiled and waved. He raised his hand in acknowledgement and felt important.

His thoughts turned to the coloured cob, watching traffic to while away the time. He doubted whether anyone noticed it and waved. *Swish! Swish! Swish!* What a bleak existence.

"Slow down to a walk," Malc said. "We want to take the next right, where that signpost is."

The horses slowed to a walk.

"Okay, road's clear. You can make the turn now if you're quick," Malc said.

Joe eased back on the right rein.

The horses went willingly, aware that it was the way home. Velvet began to forge ahead.

"Steady, Velvet, there's a girl," he crooned, still daydreaming.

"Shorten your reins, boy," Malc ordered. "It's downhill here, so you'll need them shorter than that – much shorter!"

Joe struggled to make his reins short enough. The Shires were trotting now and the traces were slack. They weren't pulling the cart any more – the cart was pushing them.

Velvet broke into a canter, really taking a hold, and Sherman cantered to keep up. It felt as if they were starting to race each other. Joe panicked. How could he have lost control so quickly?

Malc grabbed the reins. "Steady!" he commanded. "Walk!"

Within a few strides the horses were walking again. Steamy sweat rose from their unclipped coats.

"Sorry," Joe said. "I didn't realise—"

"My fault for not warning you," Malc replied. "When the cart rolls downhill it gets closer to the horses, so you need to shorten your reins and ask them to hold it back with the breeching – the straps around their behinds. They're your braking system, see?"

Joe looked, and saw that the breeching straps were tight against the horses' bottoms as they walked along.

"Here you are," Malc said, handing Joe the reins once more. "And watch Velvet – she's a devil for hurrying home."

Joe was determined not to make any more mistakes and gave the Shires his full attention.

*

It wasn't until Chris was driving him home that Joe remembered the coloured cob. As they approached its field he could see it hadn't moved much.

"Oh! Can you stop?" he asked.

Chris screeched to a halt. "What's up?"

"I'm worried about that horse," Joe said, pointing. The field looked worse in the fading light. "The piebald cob over there."

Chris drove his van onto the verge, but looked reluctant. "Quickly, then. It'll be dark soon, and we've both got animals to look after at home."

A lovely warm fug had been developing in the van. Joe got out into the freezing gloom, wondering why he hadn't kept quiet. After all, cars were driving past all the time and there were several houses dotted nearby. If there really was a problem somebody would have noticed and done something about it, wouldn't they?

Chris joined Joe, and they scrambled across an overgrown ditch, climbed gingerly over the barbed-wire fence and landed in the semi-frozen gloop on the other side.

The horse whinnied and waded towards them. Up close, it looked smaller and less chunky than Joe had imagined, more like a pony than a sturdy cob, and he could see that she was a mare.

He rummaged around in his coat pocket and gathered together a handful of pony nuts. "Hello, old girl," he said, offering them to her.

She ate them eagerly, licking up every crumb with her whiskery lips, and politely snuffled at his pockets for more.

"Sorry, that's all I've got," Joe said. He ran his hand over her two-tone winter coat. It lay curled against her skin, glued flat by water and dirt, cold and rough to the touch. She wasn't desperately thin, not like some of the rescue cases Mum took in, but he could feel her ribs.

"She's friendly enough, anyway," Chris said.

"Not surprising," Joe replied. "She must be so lonely, stuck in this awful field all by herself with nothing to do all day but stare at the traffic."

"I'll go and inspect the food and water situation," Chris said, and he squelched off.

Joe stroked the mare and talked to her. She stayed as close as possible. What a waste, he thought. Lots of people would love a gentle, friendly pony like this.

Chris came back. "The water has obviously been de-iced regularly because there are great slabs of the stuff on the other side of the fence. And she has got silage, although it isn't particularly good quality and a lot of it seems to have been trampled into the mud."

Joe pulled his phone out of his pocket. "I'll ring

Mum." His whole body was tense with cold and his feet ached. He could barely work the phone, his hands were so numb.

After a few rings Mum answered in the business-like manner she'd perfected since starting the Hidden Horseshoe.

"Mum, it's Joe."

"Oh, is everything all right?"

"Yes. Well, sort of. I mean we're fine, but there's this pony—"

Mum groaned. "Not *another* one!"

"This one's really lovely. She's so friendly, and she's in this awful muddy field without any company."

"Has she got food and water?"

"Yes, but—"

"And is she very thin?"

"No, not very, but—"

"Is she lame, ill or injured in any way?"

"I don't think so."

"Are there signs of abuse?"

"Um, not really. I mean, she loves people." Joe realised he wasn't putting a very good case forward. "But it's freezing here. There's no shelter – not even a hedge – and she hasn't got a rug or anything." His knee-caps juddered.

"I can understand your concern, Joe, but from what you've told me there's nothing we can do."

"You don't understand! It's awful! It's so wet and cold and *lonely* for her," he said desperately.

"I do understand, and I agree that the situation sounds far from ideal, but none of the things you've described are actually illegal."

"They *must* be!"

"If she were ill, very underweight or obviously in distress or danger it would be right to call the authorities, but I'm afraid it isn't a legal requirement to provide a horse with shelter, a rug, a companion or even somewhere dry to lie down."

"Oh." Joe felt utterly defeated. How could it not be wrong to keep a pony like this? It didn't make sense.

"Come on home, Joe. It doesn't sound as if there's anything we can do."

Joe went upstairs as soon as he got home, determined to work things out somehow. He turned on his computer, searched for *horse welfare law UK* and found out that Mum had been right. How could he help the lonely mare in the muddy field? He had to try.

Mum was in the kitchen cooking supper.

"Can I ring Malc?" he asked.

"Yes, okay. Do you know his number?"

"Nope, but Chris'll have it."

It turned out that Malc knew the pony well. She was called Solo, and Malc had given her owner several driving lessons in the past. "A grand pony," he said. "I think I've still got Janet's number somewhere. I'll see what I can do."

At supper Joe told his family about Solo.

"Poor pony," Emily said. "Her field sounds awful. I'd love to have a driving pony. Why don't we give her a home here?"

"Two very good reasons," Mum said. "We can't just take horses from their fields without permission and this place is full to bursting." She sighed. "I've had to turn away so many horses this winter – we simply can't help them all, however much we'd like to."

"Solo's a good name for her, isn't it?" Emily said. "All alone and lonely."

Silence, and then the phone rang. Joe rushed to answer it.

"Good news," Malc said. "Janet's delighted for you to take care of the little mare for the time being. She says if you could re-home her somewhere good and permanent, that'd be ideal because she won't be able to have her back again."

"Er. I'll have to ask." Joe's heart thumped with a mixture of elation and alarm. He'd never dreamed it would be this simple. What would Mum say? Maybe it wouldn't be so easy after all.

"Trouble is, Janet hasn't been at all well, see?" Malc went on. "She's been in and out of hospital. Her neighbour was supposed to be looking after the mare, but he's done the bare minimum as far as I can make out. It's a disgrace, and no mistake. I went to see her tonight, after you rang. Even in the dark I could tell things were bad – had a job walking into the field, it was that thick with mud . . . Are you still there?"

"Um yes. Yes, I am."

"Good. Well, I'll give you Janet's number and then maybe you or your mum can get in touch."

Joe wrote down the number, thanked Malc and rang off.

"What was that all about?" Mum asked.

"Malc's sort of arranged everything," Joe said cautiously, holding up the piece of paper he'd written on. "We've got to ring Solo's owner. It sounds like she'd be happy for us to go and pick her up."

Emily jumped up with excitement. "Hurray! Can we go now?"

Dad rolled his eyes heavenwards. "No."

"Why not?" Emily asked.

"Because it's far too late, and it's raining," Dad replied.

"Tomorrow morning, then. Ring her and tell her tomorrow morning," Emily said to Joe.

Mum cleared her throat. "Ahem! As the proprietor

of the Hidden Horseshoe, do I get a say in this matter?"

Emily gave her an angelic smile. "Only if you want to say words like *yes*."

Mum actually laughed. "Looks as if we'll have to say *yes* anyway, doesn't it? Give me the number, Joe. I'd better ring this woman and talk about minor details like a contract, money and a mutually convenient time to collect the pony."

Joe handed the piece of paper to Mum and grinned at Emily. She was definitely a useful ally sometimes.

Next morning, the whole family went to collect Solo with the horse trailer. She loaded willingly, as if she couldn't wait to get away from her field, and they were back home in no time at all.

As soon as they arrived in the yard, Solo let out a piercing whinny, which was answered several times. Overjoyed by the reaction, she whinnied again and tossed her head impatiently. Joe led her down the ramp on a long rope. She followed him eagerly, jumping the last part.

"How d'you like your new home?" Joe asked, putting his hand on her neck. It was clammy with sweat, but he didn't mind. He felt light-headed with relief that everything had gone okay. "Your name isn't so appropriate now, is it?" he said. "Soon you'll have plenty of friends."

Mum put her hand out to stroke Solo, and thought better of it. "I think the first thing to do is give her a bath and see what colour she really is. Then she can go out in the field with a rug on. We'll let her have a couple of days off and then start doing something with her. We need to get her fit and going well as soon as possible." She grinned at Joe. "Project for you in your spare time."

"Ha! Ha! Very funny," he said sarcastically, but he was grinning too.

Chapter 9

Once school started again, spare time really was a joke. There hardly seemed to be time to do anything other than school stuff. With exams approaching, the teachers started piling on the work, which seemed especially unfair when Joe wanted to concentrate on Solo and Fortune.

If ever a pony knew that she'd been saved and was grateful, it was Solo. The mud fever on her legs and rain scald on her back soon healed up and she appeared to glow with health. All the other horses loved her. She was totally passive but somehow avoided being a victim, even with the ones who were usually bullies. Mum said she could earn a living as a companion to difficult horses if nothing else, but she turned out to be a good riding pony as well. Joe had to admit he found her rather slow and unresponsive compared with the finely tuned games ponies he was used to, but otherwise he couldn't fault her. And she really was a bombproof hack. Having spent a year watching traffic go by, she wasn't afraid of anything on the road.

The most endearing thing about Solo, though, was how friendly she was. She couldn't get enough of human company. She behaved more like a dog than a pony, coming when she was called and following anyone who cared to take her for a walk. Her idea of bliss was to be groomed and fussed over.

As the mounted games team trials drew near, the pressure on Joe's time increased even more. He often practised with Emily and Caroline on Saturday mornings and Sunday afternoons, so with aikido on Saturday afternoons and homework to do as well there was little time for anything else.

The Bellsham Vale Pony Club mounted games team trials were held on the Monday of half term, in a large indoor school about an hour's drive away.

Although Mum had a trailer now, Chris offered to take Emily and Joe with Caroline in the Lucketts Farm lorry as he was going anyway.

Joe tried not to feel nervous, but it was hard, especially with everybody's expectations so high. Fortune shook with anticipation as soon as she walked into the arena and realised what was going on. He stroked her tense neck and walked her in circles, but it didn't seem to make much difference. He tried thinking of calm water, but it felt forced and Fortune seemed to know it. She only settled properly when they started racing and both of them could concentrate on the task in hand.

In the end the trial went really well, but there again it seemed to go well for everyone. There were eleven people who wanted to be in the senior team and only six places – five and a reserve – so five would be disappointed.

"Could you all line up in the centre of the arena, please?" Maria said. "Thank you so much, all of you, for coming today. The standard has been incredibly high, and I think I can safely say I've never found it so difficult to pick a team. However, after much deliberation my final decision is as follows: Caroline on Minstrel, Sarah on Flicka, Joe on Fortune, Ali on Rolo and Emily on Lightning, with Tanya and Boysie as reserve."

The new team members all grinned at each other.

"Oh, and I nearly forgot," Maria said breezily. "Joe will be the Bellsham Vale's candidate for the England team trials on the twenty-fourth of March. We all wish you the very best of luck, Joe."

There must be some mistake, Joe thought. Caroline or Sarah should be trying for the England team, not me. They're both much more experienced at mounted games and they've been in the Pony Club for ages . . . It was a huge honour, of course, but he couldn't get rid of the feeling that he didn't deserve it. He hadn't come up through the Pony Club ranks like everyone else; he'd sneaked in through the back door, first with Lightning and now Fortune, *who he hadn't even had to buy*, and stolen the ultimate prize from under his team-mates' noses. He could tell that Caroline was especially disappointed she hadn't been chosen, although she was trying to be nice about it.

In the lorry on the way home he steered the conversation towards the Prince Philip Cup. "Well, we got our dream team, didn't we?"

"Yes! I can't believe it! Prince Philip Cup here we come!" Caroline exclaimed, grinning broadly to show how happy she was.

"But we mustn't count our chickens before they're hatched," Emily said solemnly.

Joe laughed. "Spot the poultry farmer!"

"Well, for what it's worth, I think the chances of success for the Bellsham Vale have never been higher," Chris commented.

Emily grinned. "Naturally, they've got me now!" She turned to Joe. "Mum and Dad will be amazed that you've been picked for the England team!" she said.

Trust Emily! "It's only the trials," he said. "Every Pony Club branch in England can put forward a member, so there'll be lots of us battling it out for six places. Simon went last year, but he wasn't chosen and he's a brilliant rider."

"Think positive," Chris said. "You're good too. In fact," he added, "you're all excellent."

"But some more excellent than others," Caroline murmured.

Chapter 10

It was almost dark by the time Joe and Emily got home. They unboxed their ponies at Lucketts Farm and led them down the hill in the fading light, their tack still on beneath their rugs.

Mum must have heard them coming, because she came hurrying along the path from the stables to meet them.

"Guess what?" Emily called, making sure she'd be the first to tell the news, as usual. "We're both in the team, and Joe's been picked for the England trials too!"

"Oh, well done! I'm so proud of you!" Mum exclaimed, hugging each of them in turn. Then she stood back, beaming. "I've got some news as well. ET's had her foal!"

ET was a good mother – so good that they found it difficult to get a glimpse of her foal. She made sure she was between the visitors and her baby at all times.

"I can't see a thing. Can we go in?"

"No," Mum replied. "The vet said we shouldn't disturb her more than necessary – it's important to let them bond." She smiled. "He's a colt foal, in case you were wondering."

"But I was *sure* it'd be a girl! I wanted to call it Bella," Emily protested.

Mum put her arm around Emily's shoulder. "Never mind. It'll be up to ET's owner, anyway. Naming a thoroughbred is a complicated business, you know. There are lots of rules about it. All current registered racehorses have to be called something different, for a start, and you're not allowed to use famous names from the past, either."

Emily shivered suddenly. "Brrr! I'm frozen."

"Sorry, darling. Let's go inside. There'll be plenty of time to see the foal tomorrow."

Mum set off towards the house with Emily. "Come

on, Joe. Tea time!" she called over her shoulder. "Isn't it lucky I've baked a chocolate cake? There's a lot to celebrate!"

"Be with you in a minute," Joe replied. He felt cold as well, but he didn't want to leave – not yet. It was so peaceful out here, and he needed time to think. Why was the thrill he felt about being picked for the England trials tempered by the feeling that he'd taken something important from Caroline? Riding for England would be fantastic, but not if it meant losing Caroline as a friend. Why was life so *complicated*?

He rested his elbows on the stable door and peered into the shadows, happy to let the foal distract him. A light bulb hung from the ceiling, projecting a dim glow that hardly made any difference. He could tell by ET's movements and the rustling of the straw that the foal was moving around. Then there was another sound: a gentle smacking noise. As the foal suckled, the mare bent around to nuzzle his tail, turning slightly as she did so, and he came into view for the first time: dark, angular body; long forelegs; large knees; short, black, fuzzy tail swishing in ecstasy.

Joe forgot about everything that had happened that day and became lost in the moment.

ET swung round further in her eagerness to keep an eye on her baby, and he lost contact with the teats between her hind legs. He stood there, legs splayed, with creamy drops of milk clinging onto the hairs around his chin. His translucent amber eyes stared at Joe inquisitively. A diamond of white hair on his forehead shone out in the darkness.

Actually, Joe thought, it's more of a kite shape than a diamond. "Hello, Kite," he whispered.

Needless to say, the foal soon became the centre of attention. Joe loved watching him as he raced, leapt and pranced around the field. Mum said they'd have to call him something until he was named officially, and they all agreed that Kite suited him, so the name stuck. It was particularly appropriate, they realised, because it combined the first letters of his parent's names: Keep In Tempo and Ella's Tribute.

A whole week off school meant Joe was able to spend lots of time with Kite and the other horses. One thing he was very keen to try was driving Solo. The problem was that he had neither the harness nor a cart for her. Luckily it turned out Malc did, so he offered to bring them over and give Joe a lesson with Solo on the Friday of half term.

It was the most beautiful day – more like April than the end of February. Joe got up early so he could help muck out the horses and tidy up before Malc arrived. He was eager to make a good impression.

As usual, Rusty was the first on the scene when their visitor arrived.

"Ah, hello my old son," Malc said.

Joe introduced Mum, Dad and Emily, and then they carefully unloaded the cart from the trailer behind Malc's Land Rover.

"What would you like to do?" Mum asked. "Cup of coffee first, then go and see Solo? Lunch will be at around one o'clock, by the way, and I know Joe and Emily are longing to show you around the place if there's time."

Malc looked at his watch. "In that case, we'd better skip the coffee and see what Solo thinks about being driven." He smiled at Emily and Joe. "And after lunch I'd very much like to see your other horses, if I may."

Solo looked very smart in her nut-brown harness with brass buckles. It wasn't at all like the heavy horse harness Joe had become used to – much smaller, of course, but also different in design. Malc said it was called a breast harness because instead of a collar there was a padded strap that went around the pony's chest. Also, it was for a single pony with shafts on each side, rather than for a pair attached to a central pole. Added to that, it was English rather than American . . . The more Joe learned about driving, the more he realised he didn't know.

Malc stood Solo in front of the shafts and asked

her to back up, touching her shoulder to guide her.

She backed into the narrow space carefully, feeling her way step by step.

"She hasn't forgotten," Malc said. "Stand, good girl." He showed Joe how to attach the harness to the cart, and then he got into the cart while Joe stayed by Solo's head. "I doubt there'll be a problem, but lead her for a while just in case," he said.

He was right. There weren't any problems. Solo walked, trotted, stopped and stood like clockwork. She obviously enjoyed being driven because she bowled along enthusiastically, no encouragement required.

The steamy aroma of roast beef filled the kitchen. The smell always made Joe particularly hungry.

"What did you think of Solo?" Mum asked as they all sat down around the table.

"Didn't put a foot wrong. You'd have to go a long way to find a pony as good – a very long way," Malc said. "Sane and sensible as they come."

Mum looked delighted. "We'll have to start looking for a really good home for her. A place for life where she'll be loved and appreciated."

Malc nodded. "I'd be tempted if it wasn't for the fact I'm moving." It was said casually, as if everybody already knew.

Joe stared at him. "What? You're not moving from Church Farm, are you?"

Malc took some vegetables. "Afraid so. Hadn't you heard? I thought everyone knew by now."

"But *why?*" Joe asked.

"I'm going to be eighty soon. Thought it was about time to sell up and take things a bit easier." Malc paused.

Emily handed Joe the vegetables. He took a few pieces of carrot and passed the dish to Mum.

"You're not selling everything, are you?" he asked. "I mean, what about Velvet and Sherman?"

"I don't rightly know," Malc replied. He put his knife and fork down, as if he'd lost his appetite. "The sensible thing would be to sell them at the farm sale, to draw people in, but I couldn't do that to them. Wherever they go, they'll have to go together and stay together, I've told everyone that."

"Everyone?"

"Yes," Malc said. "There are a lot of people wanting them, some offering silly money too. A good working pair of Shires is hard to find nowadays. I've even had offers from abroad. Velvet's very well-bred, you see. Her sire was Black Silk, who won at Peterborough several times. Lovely stallion, he was." Malc took a mouthful of food.

Joe thought he ought to stop asking questions and

eat as well, but it was difficult to swallow.

"Where are you moving to?" Mum asked.

"One of those new bungalows on the outskirts of Coltridge." Malc made a face. "My daughter said it'd be sensible, and she's probably right. Not my cup of tea at all, but I daresay I'll get used to it."

Joe could see why Malc wouldn't be able to keep the horses if he was moving to one of those grass-free modern bungalows.

"Did you have a good ride this morning, Emily?" Mum asked, clearly wanting to let Malc eat in peace for a while.

Joe switched off and brooded over Velvet and Sherman. He'd felt so pumped up with pride when Solo had gone well that morning, and now he was totally deflated. It hadn't occurred to him that Malc would ever want to sell up and retire. Surely he didn't need to yet?

The conversation had switched to the story of Lightning and Lady, but Joe stayed quiet.

If only Mum and Dad could buy Velvet and Sherman, he thought. They never would, though. I've seen the prices of good working Shires in *Heavy Horse World*. They'd be expensive to keep as well. Malc says they eat a bale of hay a day in the winter. Everything costs more, from their shoes upwards. It's hopeless. He chased a piece of carrot around the plate with his fork, and eventually squashed it in gravy and left it there. How could everyone else chat away as if nothing was wrong? Velvet and Sherman were going to be sold, and there was nothing he could do about it.

Pudding was apple crumble and custard – Joe's favourite. Apparently it was Malc's favourite too, or maybe he was being polite. The conversation dipped in and out of different subjects, but the farm sale and the Shires weren't mentioned again.

"Where would you like to go first?" Emily asked as she got up from the kitchen table. They didn't have long to show Malc around because he had to get back to look after his animals.

"Well, I'd love to see that foal you were talking about," Malc said.

ET was sometimes wary of men she didn't know, but she took to Malc and wasn't at all worried about him making a fuss of her baby.

"Beautiful colt," he said. "The mare looks far too well to be a rescue horse."

"She isn't, not really," Joe replied. "Her owner's paying for her to be on livery because he says she's much happier here than she would be at a big stud. She couldn't cope with the pressure of a racing yard when she was in training, and she was a bundle of nerves when she first came to us, but she's settled down a lot now. I think she feels at home here." He stroked her neck. She stood like a beautiful sculpture: head erect, ears pricked and eyes deep and dark, gazing into the distance. All-seeing, all-knowing.

"The look of eagles," Malc said, smiling. "I didn't realise you had liveries as well."

"Yes, that was how we started off, taking in liveries for rehab."

"Mostly lame ones, but some nutty ones too," Emily added.

"Not always," Joe said firmly. "Sometimes their owners send them here because they're going away on holiday or moving house – all sorts of reasons. Bubble and Squeak have been here for almost a year, and there's nothing wrong with them. Their owner wants them handled well before they go to a top carriage-driving place to learn scurry driving."

Malc looked thoughtful.

"Would you like to see our big stable barn? It's state-of-the-art," Emily said proudly.

Malc smiled. "I'd like that very much, as long as it won't take too long. My animals will wonder where I've got to."

Joe thought of Sherman and Velvet waiting patiently for their tea by the gate into the yard at Church Farm, oblivious to the changes in store.

"This is Autumn," Emily said as they walked through the barn. "Isn't she beautiful? She's an Arab. She used to do a lot of long-distance riding, but she kept going lame so she's come here for Chris to make her hooves better." She made it sound so easy – like waving a magic wand rather than lots of hard work. "And this is Tyler."

Tyler lifted his head out of the manger and made a vile face, nostrils pinched and ears pinned back.

"He isn't as bad as he was, but he's still funny about food," Emily said. "Debbie owns him. He was horrid when he came – took chunks out of anyone who passed by his stable door – but he's become much nicer, especially when he's outside. Odd, isn't it? He's lovely to ride, but he doesn't like anyone near him in the stable unless he knows them well. Nellie says he's probably had a bad experience."

"More than likely," Malc agreed.

Mum came into the barn, leading Fortune and Lightning.

Malc admired both ponies and then said, "I really must be going. Thank you so much for a thoroughly enjoyable day. I was wondering whether I might be able to have a quick word, Jackie?"

Mum looked thoughtful. "Er, yes, of course." She turned to Joe and Emily. "Go and fetch some more horses, could you?"

Joe wondered what the "quick word" would be about, but when they got back to the barn with Lady and Solo, Mum and Malc were all smiles.

"It looks as if we'll have two more horses at the Hidden Horseshoe before long," Mum announced. "Malc has asked us to look after Velvet and Sherman for him."

"Brill!" Emily gasped.

"You mean look after them until they're sold?" Joe asked.

"No, look after them for ever – or at least for as long as I'm around – as liveries, like ET," Malc said. He went to Solo and stroked her. "Strange how things turn out, eh? I never wanted to sell Velvet and Sherman, but I didn't think there was any alternative until I came here today, so I've got you to thank for that, Joe."

Joe felt his throat becoming tight with emotion. He stroked the other side of the pony's neck. "Solo's the one. She's the one we should be thanking," he said.

Chapter 11

J oe had never felt so anxious about a competition, not even the Prince Philip Cup. He'd be representing the Bellsham Vale by himself at the England team trials tomorrow. What an awesome responsibility. Nervous energy fuelled his tack-cleaning efforts. His saddle became so shiny that he could almost see his face in it.

He gathered up Fortune's girth, stirrups and snaffle bit and headed for the house, running through a mental list of all the things he needed to take. Maria had said that although the contestants tomorrow would be anonymous, it helped to catch the judges' eye if you wore your Pony Club's colours, especially if your branch had done well in the Prince Philip Cup. So he was going to wear a green sweatshirt and Fortune was going to have a green numnah and browband. Her girth was white – or it would be once it had taken a ride in Mum's washing machine – and the bits and stirrup irons were destined for the dishwasher. If he got them going quickly Mum would never know. She wasn't as relaxed about that sort of thing as Caroline's mum, who often put horse stuff in the washing machine and dishwasher . . . Caroline. Why couldn't he stop thinking about her? He set the washing machine and dishwasher going on short cycles and went upstairs to check Facebook. Messages from Martin, Darren, Harry and Ali, but nothing from Caroline. He looked at her page. She'd gone on the school skiing trip, and there were lots of snowy photos, including one of her in a blue ski suit with some mountains in the background and another of her in a group hug with some friends, smiling. Always smiling . . .

Joe didn't find it too difficult to get up at five o'clock the following morning. He'd been awake anyway.

Most of the horses and ponies were dozing when he went into the barn, but Fortune was wide awake.

Maybe she'd figured out there was something up yesterday when he'd spent ages grooming her. He hoped she hadn't had a sleepless night too.

She picked at her unusually early breakfast while Joe gave her a final brush and sponged away some greenish-brown stable stains on her legs. Grey ponies were certainly much more difficult to keep clean.

Mum tried to get Joe to eat some toast before they set off. He nibbled at it and sipped the strong, sweet tea she'd made, but he soon escaped back to the stables again and prepared Fortune for the journey.

She became agitated when Joe started to put her long, padded travel boots on, and as he did up her tail guard she released some loose dung, which he narrowly avoided. She was definitely on high alert – sure she was going somewhere now.

"Okay?"

Joe looked round to see Nellie, and felt comforted by her presence. "Oh, hi. You're up early."

She smiled. "Speak for yourself. Nervous?"

He nodded.

"Remember to breathe and relax." She held out a pink envelope. "Here you are. Sorry about the colour. It's the thought that counts."

"Er, thanks." Joe opened it up and pulled out a card. It had a picture of a horseshoe on it and GOOD LUCK in bold letters, and although the design was rather girlish at least the shoe had seven holes – a proper lucky horseshoe. He opened the card and read Nellie's distinctive scrawl:

With Every Good Wish,
Nellie

"Thanks very much," he said, putting the card in his jacket pocket. He looked at his watch: a quarter to six. Time to go.

With Nellie's help, Fortune walked into the trailer without a moment's hesitation. However, as soon as the ramp had been closed she began to whinny and stomp.

"Let's get going – give her something else to think about," Mum said, getting into the driver's seat and winding down the window. "Bye, Nellie. Thanks for taking care of everything! Bye!"

Travelling to a mounted games event without any of his friends was an odd sensation for Joe. The journey seemed to go on for ever, especially as Mum was nervous about towing the trailer such a long way from home and insisted on driving without any music or other distractions. He checked his phone regularly, and found "good luck" texts from Maria, Martin, Ali, Sarah, Emily and Chris.

Eventually they arrived at the equestrian centre where the trials were taking place.

Joe was surprised by how calm he felt as he unloaded Fortune and got her ready. Now that he was there it didn't seem so bad, and there was something liberating about being by himself – being an anonymous contender rather than a member of a team. He decided to do his best and enjoy himself.

Fortune understood exactly what was going on, and her enthusiasm was infectious. As soon as Joe started the first race they both became charged with excitement.

There were nine races in all – ball and cone, bending, bottle, old sock, pony prep, rope, stepping stones, sword and two flag – and there were too many contestants to count. Joe recognised a few of them, but most were strangers with expressionless faces, identifiable only by the numbers they wore.

It didn't take long for Joe to realise he was thoroughly enjoying himself. Fortune willingly responded to the slightest cue – even a thought or a shift of his weight in the saddle. He lost track of time as he was directed to various races with different competitors in each. Finally, in the middle of the afternoon, the helpers began to pack up the equipment and the riders were asked to assemble for the results.

The gentleman who seemed to be in charge of the event gave the usual sort of speech thanking the helpers and contestants and saying how high the standard had been and how difficult it had been for the judges to come to a decision. He explained that they'd chosen eight riders in total: five team members, the reserve and two other stand-by reserves. "So, without further ado," he said, "the England team will be numbers thirty-two, eight, twenty-one, sixty-one and twenty-seven."

Joe wanted to laugh; it sounded as if he was reading out the lottery results. The number twenty-seven rang a bell, for some reason. Why was the girl beside him smiling and whispering, "Well done"? No! Twenty-seven wasn't *his* number, was it? That couldn't be right . . .

"So to recap, with names this time, the team members are: Laura van Neumann from the Devon and Somerset, Polly Wright from the Romney Marsh, Jack Rees-Jones from the Cheshire Hunt North, Tina Drummond from the Cottesmore Hunt and Joe Williams from the Bellsham Vale."

Twenty-seven! It *was* right – he really was going to ride for England!

"Could the team members and reserves stay here for a meeting, please. The rest of you are free to go. Thank you, once again, for coming."

"England team over here, please!" somebody called.

In a daze, Joe joined his new team-mates. The words *England team* resonated in his head. *England team* . . . He wondered whether Caroline would be upset – he *so* hoped not. Mrs McCulloch would be delighted, naturally, and so would Harry, Martin, Ali, Malc, his family and everybody else who'd wished him well. Not forgetting Nellie, of course. Dear old Nellie with her horseshoe card saying *Every Good Wish* . . . A horseshoe with seven holes, every good wish, England team . . . Things were all fitting together like the final pieces of a jigsaw.

Oh – my – goodness! Joe said to himself. *England Team* is my final horseshoe wish! But instead of playing football for England I'll be *riding* for England! How amazing is that?

Chapter 12

Malc's farm sale was at the beginning of the Easter holidays, a few days after the team trials. Livestock, machinery and furniture were to be auctioned because the actual farm had already been sold to a local property developer. People came from miles around, eager for a day out with the possibility of a bargain or two.

Joe spent most of the time in the stables with Velvet and Sherman. The auctioneer had asked Malc to keep the Shires there, even though they weren't for sale, because they'd be a good attraction. He was right – a constant stream of people wanted to touch, stroke, pat and even sit on the horses. Although Velvet and Sherman usually loved attention, they retreated into their stables after a while.

The horses will have to put up with this sort of thing every day if Mum's plans to open the Hidden Horseshoe to the public go ahead, Joe realised. He wondered how much Velvet and Sherman understood about what was happening. Did they know it was their final day at Church Farm? Tomorrow they'd be coming to live at the Hidden Horseshoe. He couldn't help feeling excited about that.

Mum bought a kitchen table and a framed print of some carthorses in the furniture sale and Dad bought all sorts of things, including some harness, a plough, the hitch cart and a set of chain harrows for the horses. Nigel bought Malc's Ferguson TE20 – the tractor he'd always longed for.

By the end of the next day there was no spare shed space anywhere at Newbridge Farm. The old lean-to around the back had become home to a Ransomes single-furrow horse plough, a set of chain harrows, a hitch cart and Nigel's tractor. Sherman and Velvet had stables next to each other in the barn, and the tack room had harness as well as saddlery in it.

Joe couldn't quite believe it had happened. He kept going into the barn to check that Velvet and Sherman were still there, and the sight of them gave him a thrill every time.

Sherman settled in straight away, craning his neck over the stable door to greet anyone passing by. Joe noticed that his straw had been flattened in the night, showing he'd gone to sleep lying down. Nellie said that was a sure sign he felt at home.

Unfortunately Velvet wasn't so happy. She picked at her food, hardly drank anything, paced around her stable all night and put her ears back at any horse or pony that came near. With her heavy steel shoes she could do irreparable damage to other horses if she kicked them, so the two Shires had to be turned out by themselves in the orchard.

Joe's excitement about having the Shires at home was tempered by the fact that Solo was sent on trial for a month to a potential new home: a Riding for the Disabled centre near Bellsham. It provided both riding and driving for people with all sorts of different disabilities, and the manager was looking for an even-tempered pony. Needless to say, Solo fitted the bill exactly. Joe knew she'd be loved and well looked after there, but he still missed her.

*

Not a day went by in the Easter holidays when Joe wasn't with horses: practising mounted games with Fortune for the area competition at the end of April and the international competition in May, spending time with Kite and ET, chain harrowing the fields with Velvet and Sherman or driving them around the lanes with the hitch cart. It was a glorious spring, with hardly a drop of rain, and people started to talk about droughts and hosepipe bans.

Malc became a regular visitor to the farm. Like Nellie, he taught Joe a lot about horses. For instance, he said Joe should concentrate on ET rather than Kite. "You can overdo things handling foals, see?" he said. "Kite needs to look to his mother, not you. At this stage he'll pick up much more from ET than you'll be able to teach him. Five minutes at a time with that foal is plenty, then make a big fuss of the mare so she doesn't feel left out. I hardly handled Sherman at all when he was a young colt, but I had to work Velvet and so he tagged along. He learned the ropes before he had a single piece of harness put on him – learned from his mum. He worked out what the voice commands meant and everything. Velvet broke him in for me, more or less."

Other frequent visitors were Martin and his dad. Nigel came to work on his tractor and do odd jobs with Dad around the farm – Mum said it was "playing", but Dad insisted it was "hard work".

Martin originally tagged along to help with the tractor, but inevitably he joined in with whatever Joe was doing, which was usually something with horses. He didn't mind handling horses from the ground, but he'd never really been keen on the idea of riding them. Driving the Shires was a different matter, though, and he took to it immediately.

Joe enjoyed chain harrowing; there was something wonderfully satisfying and soothing about walking up and down a field, holding a pair of long cotton plough lines, with a wide expanse of gently clattering metal in front of him and, even further away, Velvet and Sherman walking steadily side-by-side.

He especially liked turning the horses when they reached the edge of the field. With a touch of pressure on the lines and a gentle command, "Come round", they both crossed their legs over with the elegance of dancers and ended up facing the opposite direction. Sometimes Velvet would take advantage of Joe's inexperience and would back up a step or two and put a leg over the traces.

"Her way of getting a rest," Malc said as he helped Joe to unhook the trace from the whipple-tree, push her over and do it up again the first time it happened. "Ever heard the expression 'stepping over the traces', boy?"

"Sort of means to rebel, doesn't it?"

Malc nodded. "Well, Velvet's a little too old and wise to rebel, but she's testing you to see what you're made of. You'll know what to watch for now, so you'll be able to stop her in time. Keep on practising and you'll be surprised how much you'll both improve."

He was right. By the end of the Easter holidays Velvet and Sherman were working well, and between them Joe and Martin had harrowed most of the fields.

Lots of practice also paid off for the Bellsham Vale Pony Club games team. They won the area trials at the end of the Easter holidays with several points to spare. They'd be going to the zone finals at the end of June to battle it out for a place at the Horse of the Year Show. They had high hopes; their team was stronger than ever this year.

Chapter 13

The England team had a training camp just before Royal Windsor Horse Show. That was the only chance they got to practise together. The main aim of the camp was to find out their strengths and weaknesses and to allow them to get to know each other. They were missing a week of school to take part, so although they were all prepared to work hard there was definitely a holiday feel in the air.

It was a new experience for Joe to ride with people he didn't know. How they'd got as far as the England team wasn't important; the only thing that mattered was what happened now. Nobody knew that Joe was a boy from Birmingham who, not so long ago, hadn't even realised people did mounted games. He liked that. It made a refreshing change.

Laura was the only team member Joe had met before. She'd ridden for the Devon and Somerset branch at the Horse of the Year Show. He particularly remembered her pony, Sundance, because she was a brilliant games pony and looked similar to Lightning: chestnut body, flaxen mane and tail and white blaze.

The others were Polly, with an experienced grey mare called Mia, Jack and his fiery liver-chestnut gelding Woody, and Tina with her nippy roan gelding Levi. Jack was the joker of the pack, rather like a hyperactive version of Martin, and he and Joe automatically became good mates.

By the time they moved on to Windsor they were no longer strangers; they were a team.

Royal Windsor Horse Show was different from the Horse of the Year Show. There was much more space, for a start, with green trees and grass all around and Windsor Castle ever-present in the background.

Although the International Mounted Games was a serious competition, everyone was out to have a good time. This was a once-in-a-lifetime challenge, and all the more fun for it.

Joe wore his England team sweatshirt with pride: white with red writing, and a jacket to match. It was extraordinary to think he was representing his country. It really was a wish come true.

The last day of the show was a Sunday. The place was buzzing, and the showground filled with spectators much earlier than usual so their early morning warm-up session in the car park field was cut short. It was probably just as well, because both the ponies and their riders were feeling tired. The mounted games teams had been battling it out for three days now, and it was still impossible to tell who would win.

The Welsh had won the competition that morning, with the English a close second. As they returned to the stables, Joe got a text from Emily:

saw u riding u were brill! Em xxx

Joe grinned. Caroline would have seen too. Maria had hired a minibus so that members of the Bellsham Vale Pony Club could come to the final day of the show.

Joe was jittery with nerves. He told himself it was because of the final, and tried to take his mind off things by grooming Fortune, but she picked up on his mood and became agitated, so he leaned on Woody's stable door and talked to Jack.

"Hi, big brother!" Emily cried, rushing headlong at

Joe and giving him a hug. She had several plastic bags in her hands, which thumped around him.

Joe hugged her back. "How did you get in here?"

"Mum got me a pass – look, I'm official."

."Hm, kind of you to buy so many presents for me."

Emily gave him her best little girl smile, and pulled a pink fluffy numnah out of the largest bag. "Tadaa! Thought you'd like it!"

Joe recoiled in horror. "Ugh! That's revolting!"

"Is it alive?" Jack asked, coming to the stable door.

Joe laughed. "No, it died a horrible death. You're not going to make Lightning wear that, are you?"

"Of course. It'll look gorgeous on her." Emily reached into another bag and extracted a diamante browband. "Especially with this."

Joe snorted. "Poor pony. How undignified! She's a pony, not a Barbie doll, you know."

"That's the trouble with boys – no sense of fun," Emily said, stuffing everything back into the bag. "Oh, before I forget, Tracey asked me to say good luck from everyone at Lucketts Farm. They've all gone to a point-to-point today because Chris is riding Chocolate Buttons."

"Oh, right."

Emily beamed at him. "But loads of us are here, and we'll be cheering you on. I'll wave my pink numnah, so you can see where we are."

"Don't you dare!"

Emily gave him another mischievous grin. "Got to go. They're all waiting for me outside. Byee! Good luck!"

That afternoon, just before the finals, Joe was about to turn his phone off and put it away in a safe place when it buzzed in his hand. He glanced down:

osu! c x

For a moment the most important thing to Joe was the c x at the end, but then he felt a surge of nostalgia as he re-read osu! It had become the secret message of support between him and Caroline before mounted games competitions – an aikido pledge to do their best, no matter what. She'd remembered! His spirits soared and he felt charged with energy. He replied quickly:

tnx. osu choc butns 2! Joe

He paused, his thumb hovering . . .

x

and then he went to join the others.

The final competition took place in the Castle Arena. To begin with the teams cantered five-abreast around it, with the rider in the middle of each team carrying their country's flag.

Joe felt incredibly proud to be carrying the English flag, even if it was pretty nerve-wracking.

Caroline's text lodged in Joe's mind, creating a powerful mixture of joy and determination. All his senses focused on the moment. He wasn't even conscious of what he was doing when he accelerated, slowed, turned, dismounted, vaulted or handled the equipment – in the same way that he didn't think about walking, talking or eating. All the things he did when riding came naturally now. Nellie had been right: Fortune had allowed him to take his horsemanship to another level. Feel had become far more important than technique.

The races flew by so fast that it was quite a shock when the commentator announced the final contest – the big sack race – and confirmed that Wales was still in the lead with England only two points behind.

Joe felt exhausted. It had been a hot day and he'd just run a long way, bent double and dressed up in a furry suit, as the back end of a cow. Sometimes he wondered about the sanity of the people who made up Pony Club games.

There was a slight feeling of déjà vu as he prepared to line up on foot for the start of the big sack race. It reminded him of the Prince Philip Cup final when the Bellsham Vale had come a close second to the Angus team. Would it happen this time as well?

Would Wales beat them by a few points?

Joe's legs trembled with fatigue. The other end of the arena appeared to be much further away than usual. How could that be possible? He imagined Caroline smiling and saying, "*Osu!*"

They'd lined up now, ready for the flag to be lowered. Joe concentrated hard . . .

The flag went down, and Joe ran, his legs working like pistons, one in front of the other, on and on, pounding along beside the galloping ponies . . . Wait for the girls to dismount, then run again, back to the sack . . . Get in, hold the corner and jump, jump, jump, jump, breathe-deep, one, *two*, one, two, *o-su*, *o-su*, breathe-jump, breathe-jump, *o-su*, *o-su*, horse-shoe, horse-shoe, jump, jump, *o-su*, *o-su*, horse-shoe, horse-shoe, Eng-land, Eng-land . . .

The crowd was chanting it: "*England! England!*" Cheering on the home team. "*England! England!*" The chanting became louder.

Every breath seared into his parched lungs, but he kept going – the roar of the crowd giving him the willpower to carry on: "*England! England! England! England! England! England! England! Hurray!*" Applause echoed around the arena as Joe, Jack, Tina and Polly jumped over the finish line and collapsed in a heap.

"And so," the announcer said, "the final result of the DAKS International Pony Club Mounted Games

Competition is as follows: first place England, second Wales, third the Republic of Ireland, and joint fourth Northern Ireland and Scotland."

With legs like jelly, Joe got up and hugged his team-mates. They'd won! Incredible! *They'd won!*

By the time they'd all gathered their breath and their ponies, the arena had been made ready for the prize-giving.

"And now His Royal Highness the Duke of Edinburgh will present the prizes," the announcer said.

It was difficult to take everything in: the applause from the crowd, Prince Philip talking to Joe and presenting rosettes and a trophy to the team, the band playing, cantering in a lap of honour around the arena with their flag held aloft and the crowd clapping in time to the music, a final victorious gallop down the centre, signing each other's shirts, lots of hugs and promises to remain friends forever.

Joe had had the time of his life, but he was ready for home.

His head lolled against the back of the car seat as Mum drove along the motorway, and he gave up trying to keep his eyes open. A feeling of contentment came over him. All his wishes really had come true, one way or another. He smiled dreamily. Whatever happened, he'd never forget the time when he rode for England and won . . .

Chapter 14

I n the days that followed it poured with rain, and then the days turned into weeks and months. It was almost as if it couldn't remember how to stop raining. Gymkhanas, school sports days, village fetes and other outdoor events had to be cancelled as the summer term drew to a close.

The only riding competition in Joe's diary that went ahead as planned was the zone finals of the Pony Club mounted games. It was a tough contest, but Joe's winning streak continued and the Bellsham Vale team scraped through. They'd be going to the

Horse of the Year Show in October to compete for the Prince Philip Cup!

The never-ending rain became a major topic of conversation for everyone, and floods were a regular news item all of a sudden.

"We won't be flooded, will we?" Emily asked anxiously one night when they were watching TV. "Only, Vicky at school says her granny remembers this whole valley flooding and the old bridge getting washed away. She says our farm used to be called Bridge Farm but the owners changed it to Newbridge Farm when the new bridge was built."

Dad gave her a reassuring smile. "Don't worry, darling, it's one of the first things we looked into when we saw how near this place was to the river. There's been a lot of money spent on flood defences, and we were assured there hasn't been any flooding since then." He switched channels. "Here, let's watch *The Simpsons* instead."

It was an article in *Heavy Horse World* that gave Joe the idea of riding Sherman. Apparently Shires and Clydesdales were excelling in all sorts of equestrian sports, from hunting to dressage, and several places were offering trekking holidays with heavies. There'd even been a charity race for Shires at a race meeting recently, with proper jockeys on board.

To begin with Joe simply climbed onto Sherman's back in the stable, using the mobile stepladder that was kept in the tack room. The big horse kept munching hay without a pause, as if he hadn't even noticed. It was odd, but in a way he was far less daunting to sit astride than a lanky, razor-sharp thoroughbred. It was rather like being on a large, sturdy pony – safe and solid, with plenty of mane to hold on to.

Before long, Joe was hopping onto the Shire's broad back at every opportunity. Sherman's walk was a real surprise. He'd expected it to be clumsy, especially compared with Fortune, but it was so smooth that he could hardly feel the motion at all. And riding with a head collar was no problem because Sherman was used to voice commands. His only fault – if you could call it that – was he was so well-trained that if he was set on a course he'd keep going at the same pace until he was told to stop, so if Joe forgot to give him any instructions they were liable to end up in a fence or hedge.

Of course, Emily didn't want to be excluded from the fun. Soon she was climbing on behind Joe, and they led Velvet in and out from Sherman's back. If Caroline was around, she hopped on too.

Joe's first proper ride on Sherman happened

almost by accident. Caroline and Emily were going out for a quick hack with Chocolate Buttons and Lightning. They asked Joe to go with them, but Fortune had just been given her tetanus and flu vaccination so she needed the day off.

"Ride something else, then," Caroline suggested. "You're spoilt for choice here."

"Hardly," Joe replied. "Most of them can't be ridden for one reason or another."

"How about Lady?"

"She's just had her jab too."

"Well, Sherman hasn't. Ride him."

Joe laughed. "We haven't got a saddle that'll fit him, and his bridle has blinkers."

"So? We're only going round the block, and we needn't go fast."

Joe looked up at her sitting on Chocolate Buttons. She'd grown much taller recently. A thoroughbred suited her.

"Come on, Joe, it'll be fun," Emily chipped in.

"All right, let's do it," Joe said, already heading towards the tack room, fizzy inside at the thought of taking Sherman out.

The high spirits of Buttons and Lightning rubbed off on Sherman, and he walked with a definite swagger as they set off down the road.

Crossing over the bridge, they looked warily at the

river gushing beneath it. The fields, usually sun-drenched at this time of year, were shaded by a dark grey sky. They trotted up the hill towards the gate onto the bridlepath where Fortune had encountered the pheasants. Sherman's trot was long, level and incredibly comfortable, thank goodness.

"You should come to a Pony Club rally with him, you know," Caroline said as they walked along the bridle path.

Joe grinned. "Can you imagine the comments I'd get?"

Caroline giggled. "Yes, but they'd soon shut up once they saw how good he was, wouldn't they? I bet he'd do a pretty cool dressage test."

They walked down the hill and cautiously negotiated the wooden bridge at the bottom. The warm, wet weather had made it green and slippery, and turbulent brown water forced its way underneath. There wasn't much space left between the river and the planks.

The rain, which had held off for at least an hour, started again. Swollen drops fell from billowing clouds and something suspiciously like thunder rumbled in the distance.

"Oh no, we're going to get soaked," Caroline said.

Joe looked at the long, grassy hill stretching up towards Lucketts Farm – one of their favourite gallops. "Not if we hurry."

"Race you!" Emily shouted.

A moment later Sherman, Chocolate Buttons and Lightning were galloping up the field to Lucketts Farm side-by-side; carthorse, racehorse and games pony – an unlikely trio of friends.

Chapter 15

The incessant rain put an end to most of the Pony Club fixtures at the beginning of the summer holidays, including camp. Joe was glad of a break in some ways. It gave him more time to relax and do different stuff like going fishing with Martin. They had good waterproof coats and trousers, and Rusty didn't seem to care how wet he got. In fact, the rain was actually an advantage in some ways because it scared off all but the keenest fishermen, leaving plenty of space around the lake. The boys managed to find a perfect spot, and had great success with a new kind of buzzer they'd invented while experimenting with fly-tying. It had strands of horsehair wrapped around the shank of the hook and then coated with varnish. There were three kinds, depending on whose mane had been used: brown Lightning Buzzers, black Velvet Buzzers and grey Fortune Buzzers. Martin joked that perhaps horses were useful after all, although they both knew how much he liked the Shires.

After a while, though, the rain also affected fishing as the lake filled to overflowing, and Joe found himself spending more time with Chris, accompanying him on his rounds or watching him work in his forge at Lucketts Farm.

One afternoon, as Joe was looking out of the kitchen window at the washed-out landscape and summoning the enthusiasm for another ride in the pouring rain, Chris rang.

"I'm making some new shoes for Velvet and Sherman. Want to come and take a look?" he asked.

Joe leapt at the chance.

"Want to make one?" Chris asked as soon as he arrived.

Joe smiled. "Okay, then." Chris had allowed him to make small, relatively simple things before, but he couldn't believe he was actually going to make a proper shoe – something really useful – something Sherman or Velvet might eventually wear.

"First I'll make one, so you can see what to do. Here, put on this apron and some goggles."

Chris made a shoe, giving a running commentary all the way through. It was fascinating to watch as the dull metal bar was gradually transformed into a horseshoe. He emphasised the importance of getting mild steel to exactly the right heat so it could be worked easily – yellow heat for shaping and red heat for punching holes.

It took him about a quarter of an hour to make the shoe from start to finish. "Okay, your turn now," he said to Joe. "Don't worry, I'll help you."

Everything was hot, heavy and unwieldy. Joe concentrated as hard as he could on what he was being told to do. He worked cautiously, thinking about every move, but even so Chris had to step in repeatedly to steer him in the right direction. Because he was working so carefully, the steel bar lost its heat before he'd done much. It had to be reheated all the time, so he made slow progress.

After frequent trips to and from the furnace, he at last had a toe bend of about ninety degrees in the centre of the bar, and it was time to forge the outside heel. This needed different hammer skills because the blows had to be directed into the bar so the heel was shaped but not drawn out. Each blow sent shockwaves up his left arm and through his body.

Joe's arms and shoulders ached, his hand smarted from holding the hammer tightly and he felt sweaty all over, but he wasn't even halfway there yet. The air inside the forge had become humid, despite the open door. Outside the rain splashed down.

Joe set to work shaping the outside branch, turning it gradually using the beak of the anvil, beginning at the toe end and taking the bend steadily towards the heel . . . As the shoe appeared he sensed a feel and rhythm in his work and began to enjoy himself. The metal was no longer an alien substance that had to be bashed into submission; it was going to be a horseshoe – a thing of beauty developing before his eyes.

Chris punched the nail holes into the shoe, four for the outside branch, because it was a particularly skilled job and he said Joe deserved a breather. Then Joe took over to shape the inside branch. Chris punched three holes in that, drew out the toe clip, let Joe hot-rasp the heels and the shoe was complete. It had taken nearly two hours.

"Well done! Your first horseshoe, and a difficult one at that," Chris said.

Joe ran a hand across his sweaty forehead. "Piece of cake," he said with a wry smile.

Chris grinned. "Good. So you'll make the other six shoes for me, will you?"

Joe laughed. "Depends when you want them by – Christmas?"

Chapter 16

The heavy rain soaked Joe to the skin as he ran home. To begin with it was refreshing after being in the forge, like swimming after sunbathing, but by the time he reached the house he was the sort of cold that only a hot bath can put right.

He went into the bathroom, peeled off his clothes and sank gratefully into the bath. His shoulders and back began to relax as the water warmed his tired muscles.

Mum knocked on the door. "Joe? Don't be long. Dad and I both need the bathroom. We're going out, remember?"

"Okay," Joe replied. He'd forgotten that Mum and Dad were off to Tracey's birthday party tonight: a trip to the theatre in Bellsham.

"Oh, and Joe?"

"Yup?"

"Caroline's coming to stay the night because Angus is with his auntie. Richard arranged it so Tracey can have a proper break. I've made up your bed with clean sheets for Caroline, and you and Martin can sleep in the spare room."

Joe dried himself quickly and dashed into his bedroom, thinking *Caroline's coming to stay in here! How on earth will I get it tidy in time?*

He did the best he could, and when he heard Caroline arrive he shoved everything else under the bed, out of sight, so that the cardboard box with the old horseshoe in it was shunted against the wall with a *Clunk!*

"Wow! You look lovely!" Emily said when Mum and Dad came downstairs.

"Very smart," Caroline agreed. "I love that dress."

Mum smiled. "Thanks."

Dad collected the car keys from the dresser. "You know our mobile numbers, so if anything happens give us a ring," he said.

"All the horses are out, by the way," Mum added. "They couldn't stay in forever, and the forecast looks better for tonight – thundery downpours further north but only scattered showers for us. There's a list of which horses are in which fields on the board in the tack room, in case you need it for any reason. There's a casserole and baked potatoes in the oven. What else?"

"It's okay, Mum. Go on – go! And have a great time," Joe said.

Mum gave him a hug. "I forget how grown up and sensible you are."

Martin snorted.

Mum patted him on the cheek. "Unless you're around, of course, Martin the Menace."

She kissed Emily. "Bye, darling. Be good." And she smiled at Caroline. "Make sure they behave themselves, won't you?"

"Oh no, you can't ask me to be responsible for this lot," Caroline said. "That's an impossible task!"

Dad helped Mum into her coat and, after some final goodbyes, they set off.

Emily looked at the kitchen clock. "Hurray, nearly time for *Fame and Fortune!*"

They quickly served up the casserole and took their plates into the sitting room so they could eat in front of the TV.

"Ice-cream, anyone?" Joe asked when they'd all

finished eating. As he got up to collect the plates, the TV went fuzzy and the lights flickered off and on. There was a low rumble overhead.

"Uh-oh," Emily said. "Should we check whether the computer's unplugged?"

"Yes. You do that and I'll go and find Rusty. He hates thunder."

But before he could do anything, the TV shut down. The room was pierced with light and almost instantaneously thunder boomed through the house.

Emily screamed and clung to Caroline.

"Wait here. I'll get Rusty," Joe said. "Unplug the TV and any other electrical stuff you can find."

Joe found Rusty in his bedroom, cowering under the duvet, and managed to man-handle him downstairs into the kitchen.

The storm raged around the house and rain drummed against the windows.

"What about the horses, Joe?" Emily cried. "They're all out in this! *What shall we do*?"

Joe went to the back door, opened it and stepped outside. Warm, fat raindrops splashed against him. He peered into the murky twilight. Suddenly a bolt of lightning lit the landscape, just long enough for Joe to see that some of the fields close to the river had a silvery sheen. They glimmered momentarily, then faded to grey again. His stomach contracted with horror. "Water!" he cried. "The fields are flooding – they're covered with water!"

"We need Mum and Dad!" Emily wailed.

"Yes, we'd better ring them," Joe said. He tried Mum's mobile, then Dad's, but they were both on answerphone.

Caroline and Martin both tried their parents' phones, but got a similar response.

"What about Chris?" Joe asked.

Caroline dialled his number. "Answerphone as well." She put her hand on her forehead. "Oh, of course! They'll be in the theatre by now."

Joe swore. "*And* Nellie's away."

"Yes, she's staying with her sister." Emily looked close to tears.

"We'll just have to leave messages and hope they pick them up in the interval," Joe said. "You do that, and stay here to look after Rusty and answer the phone, and I'll go and see how deep the water is."

"I'll come with you, Joe," Caroline said.

"Great," he replied. "Thanks."

"So will I," Martin said.

"I'm not staying here by myself!" Emily squeaked.

"Um, d'you mind keeping her company, Martin?" Joe asked.

Martin nodded, although he didn't look too happy about it.

Joe handed Caroline some waterproofs and found some for himself. Then he took a torch from the shelf by the back door. "Okay," he said. "Let's go."

Chapter 17

J oe read from the board in the tack room, trying hard to stop his mounting panic from showing. "ET, Kite, Lightning, Fortune and Lady are all in Meadow Field – that's the long, thin one next to the river. They're the most at risk! Tyler and three others are in Tythe Field – the next one up – so we'll have to bring them in first to get them out of the way."

"Come on, we'd better hurry," Caroline said, passing him a handful of head collars and keeping some for herself.

Tyler and his companions were all by the gate,

shivering and agitated, so Joe and Caroline took them to their stables and set off again.

Rain fell steadily, but they hardly noticed. They were more concerned about the ground underfoot as it became increasingly soggy. Puddles turned into pools and then running water. They squelched . . . sloshed . . . waded, each step taking them deeper.

At last Joe could see the gate into Meadow Field. Only the top three rungs were showing. He'd hoped that the horses would be there, waiting, but there was no sign of them. The flood-water was above his knees now and the current was much stronger, dragging him sideways. He felt something bump against his arm. It was Caroline, reaching out to steady herself. He took her hand and they made it to the gate together. Once there, they clung to the gatepost, getting their breath back while the dark, menacing water churned around them.

There was still no sign of the horses. "For-tune! Light-ning!" Joe called.

With an urgent whinny and lots of splashing, ET appeared – eyes bulging, rug askew, mane and forelock slick against her wet skin.

"Good girl!" Joe said, trying to sound soothing through chattering teeth. "We'll soon have you out of here."

A high-pitched sound came from somewhere to

the right. It sounded like Kite's whinny.

ET responded with a frantic reply and charged off again, her rug trailing through the water.

Joe and Caroline peered into the semi-darkness, but they couldn't see anything.

"There's a mound of higher ground further along the hedge. I expect they've all taken refuge there," he said.

"I hope so," Caroline replied. "Come on, let's get this gate open."

They tried everything, but they couldn't do it. The gate just wouldn't open! The force of the water pressing against it was too great. Lifting it off its hinges was impossible too.

The helplessness of the situation was exhausting, but Joe couldn't give up, not with the horses trapped on the other side.

"At least we can climb the gate and check that they're okay," Caroline said.

"Good idea," Joe replied.

They only realised how much the hedge had been sheltering them from the strength of the current when they landed in the field. Caroline fell almost immediately, gasping and choking.

Joe caught hold of her and dragged her to her feet, nearly losing his footing in the process. He remembered what Sensei Radford had said about water: "It is a vital element that can both nurture life and cause death and destruction."

Death and destruction . . .

"It's no good. We'd better go back," he gasped.

"But we can't!"

"We've got no choice. It's crazy to put ourselves in danger too." He hated admitting defeat, but there really was no option.

They struggled back over the gate, trembling with cold and fatigue, and headed back to relatively dry land. This time they automatically held hands as they pushed through the swirling liquid.

"It'll be easier if we move together, like doing the big sack race," Caroline said.

"One, two, one two," Joe said, and Caroline joined in. "One, two, one, two."

Without thinking, Joe started saying, "*Osu, osu,*" instead.

Caroline giggled. "I always say that in my head when I'm doing the sack race, do you?"

"Yes." Joe paused. "That text you sent me before the finals at Windsor . . . It meant a lot to me, you know."

Caroline squeezed his hand. "Good. Um, I'm sorry I was so weird about you being chosen for the England team. I'd set my heart on it, I suppose – following in Chris' footsteps and all that – but I know I wouldn't have been brave enough. I'd have been way too nervous. I always seem to go to pieces when it matters most."

"No you don't. How about just now? You were the brave one. You wanted to carry on."

"That was different."

"I don't see how. You're a brilliant rider. All you need is faith in yourself."

The water was around their ankles now. Caroline turned and gave him a cold, wet, waterproof-clad hug. "Friends?" she asked.

"Of course. Always, no matter what."

Even in the dark, Joe could see she was smiling her special, wonderful smile.

They hurried towards the house, still holding hands.

Emily was almost hysterical when Joe and Caroline explained about the gate. "Nobody's rung! Their phones are still turned off. I've left lots of messages. You'd have thought they'd at least check!" she sobbed.

"How about calling the emergency services? I mean, this really is an emergency," Caroline said.

"I've already phoned them, but the lady said they're flat out rescuing people, and that's their priority. This seems to have taken everyone by surprise," Martin said. He wasn't his usual jokey self at all.

Joe glanced around the kitchen in despair. Everything looked ridiculously dry and normal. It was almost possible to forget the flood-water creeping up the hill outside. Almost.

What on earth could they do? The emergency services weren't interested and they didn't have anything that could pull a gate down. The Ferguson tractor would be no good; it was too small and low to the ground. They really needed one of those monster tractors from Lucketts Farm – some serious horsepower . . . *Horsepower!* He grabbed the phone, dialled Malc's number and felt a wave of relief when his familiar, unhurried voice answered.

"Malc! It's me, Joe!"

"How are you, boy? I've heard tell the river's flooded. The bridge here at Coltridge has been swept away, you know."

"Really? No, I didn't know that."

"Proper stranded, we are," Malc said. He sounded as if he was enjoying the drama.

"Yes, we are too. It's awful. The fields are flooding, and some of the horses are trapped in Meadow Field, next to the river. We can't get the gate open to let them out. So I was thinking, what about using Sherman? I could ride him through the water to the gate, if you reckon he could do it."

"Don't see why not. Put the traces on, same as we use for harrowing, but I shouldn't bother about the whipple trees – they'll be tricky to carry. A piece of chain or a good, strong piece of rope joined to the traces should do the trick. Worth a try, eh?"

"Definitely! Thanks, Malc."

"Keep safe, boy. And good luck."

Chapter 18

J oe grabbed his riding hat, shoved it on his head and took an old coat from the rack by the back door. "I'll go straight to the field and let Sherman and Velvet in," he said. "Getting their head collars from the barn will waste time. They'll run in okay – they usually do – especially if there are a few oats in their mangers."

"We'll put some feed in, won't we, Caroline?" Emily said.

Martin followed Joe. "Thought I'd be more use coming with you," he said.

They both ran, slipping on the wet ground, the narrow beam of the torch bobbing ahead of them.

It was nearly dark now. The rain had eased slightly but thunder still rumbled around the valley and lightning danced between banks of clouds in the distance.

Joe reached the gate of the field and called, "Sherman! Velvet!" It was usually enough to bring them running, but not tonight. What was that gushing sound? Paralysed with dread, he shone the torch into the field and picked out the dark reflection of a moving mass of water. "Oh no! Even this one's flooded," he said. "In the middle there – where an old trackway used to run up to Lucketts – it's like a river!" He directed the beam upwards and caught sight of a grey shape in the distance with a shadowy form beside it. "Look! There they are!" He called the horses again, but they stayed put. "Come on," he said as he opened the gate. "We'll have to go and get them."

The temporary river was incredibly strong, but the boys ploughed on regardless and reached the horses. Velvet snorted with alarm at the drowned rats before her, but Sherman just showed mild curiosity.

"Walk on, Sherman. Walk on!" Joe commanded breathlessly, tapping his bottom.

Sherman walked on a few paces and stopped again, so Joe tried the same thing with Velvet. She kicked up her heels and trotted off, veered round and came back again.

"This is hopeless!" Martin said. "I'll go back to the stables and get some head collars."

"No, it'll take too much time! Here, take this torch so you can see your way back and give me a leg-up onto Sherman. I'll ride him through the water. Horses are much better at seeing in the dark than humans, so we'll be okay."

"But you haven't got a saddle or bridle or anything."

"Nope, but I've ridden him plenty of times with just a head collar. He knows where he's going – he just needs a bit of encouragement, that's all."

"Okay. One, two, three, hup! Good luck, mate!"

With Joe on his back, Sherman took more notice, or perhaps he understood better, because he walked, then trotted down the hill, splashed through the water and kept trotting as he went through the gate and back to the stables. After a moment's hesitation, Velvet followed. Martin, wearing a pair of ruined trainers and sodden clothes, brought up the rear.

Soon both the Shires were licking oats from their mangers while Joe and the others collected Sherman's collar and hames, trace harness and bridle, together with a long rope and some head collars for ET, Kite, Fortune, Lightning and Lady.

"There's no way you can manage all that by

yourself. I'm coming too," Caroline said.

Emily linked arms with Caroline. "And me."

"Do you think I ought to come as well?" Martin asked doubtfully as Joe harnessed Sherman. "How many people can he carry?"

"Um, he's carried the three of us several times, but four might be pushing it a bit," Joe said. Having a nervous Martin on board a massive Shire horse in a flood probably wouldn't be terribly helpful, but he didn't want to make him feel left out. "Could you man the phone? Someone ought to be doing that. And if we're not back soon, ring the emergency services."

Martin looked relieved. "Sure."

Joe led Sherman out of the barn, and Martin gave them all leg-ups before handing them the head collars and the torch. "Good luck," he said.

"Cheers, Martin!" Joe replied. "We expect hot chocolate and cake on our return."

Martin waved them off. For once he seemed lost for words.

The torch projected a jerky beam as Sherman set off down the hill with Joe in front, Emily in the middle and Caroline behind. Sheets of water spilled down the hill towards the ever-expanding flood. It was as if the whole countryside was overflowing – a massive bath with the plug in and the taps running.

As they reached the gate, Joe noticed that only two rungs were visible now. He shone the torch downwards. The current swirling around Sherman's legs seemed stronger than before. Much stronger. They'd have to do everything from Sherman's back. He guided him alongside the gate. "Caroline? If I hold him steady, can you unhook the traces and tie the rope around the end of the gate? That way we'll get the best leverage."

Sherman seemed to know how important this was. He stood as still as an island.

Now for the moment of truth, thought Joe. "Hang on really tight, and try to keep your legs up out of the way," he told the girls. "Everybody ready?"

"As ready as we'll ever be," Caroline said.

"Walk on!"

Sherman walked on, stopped abruptly, and then, without warning, heaved forwards, plunging through the inky-black water.

Joe nearly fell off sideways as the traces whipped up under his legs. He clung on to the hames valiantly, trying to ignore the pain. "Whoah! Whoah, there!"

Sherman stopped, head held high and ears back, trembling with alarm.

Joe knew Emily was still there because her arms were like a tourniquet around his stomach, but he didn't know what had happened to Caroline. "Everyone all right?"

"Yes," said Emily.

"Just about," said Caroline. "What shall we do about the gate? It's still attached to the traces – somewhere in the water behind us."

Joe bit his lip, thinking about their new dilemma. There was no way any of them could get off and undo the rope, and the traces were being pulled taut by the weight of the gate. They'd have to drag it to the water's edge. More precious time.

Once there, Caroline slid off and tried to undo the rope. "Sorry, but it's impossible!" she cried.

Joe dismounted to help, but it was no use. His numb hands wouldn't work properly and the knots were so tight that they'd become fused. "We'll have to take the harness off," he said.

They unhooked the traces with the belly band, and left a tangled mess of leather, rope and wood in the water. They left the collar on because Joe didn't want to ruin that as well. Besides, the hames made useful hooks for the head collars and gave him something to hang onto. Then Caroline gave Joe a leg-up onto Sherman before scrambling on with his help.

Soon they were heading back to the field again. Sherman plodded on as if he'd been doing this strange job all his life. They passed through the ominous gap where the gate had been. Water lapped underneath Sherman's belly.

"ET! For-tune! Light-ning!" Joe called.

Silence, apart from the patter of raindrops and the gurgling, rushing sound of the flood-water.

Emily's grip tightened. "We're too late. They've been swept away," she whispered.

Joe was thinking much the same thing, but he said, "Let's not give up yet. This is where they were before, I think," and he steered Sherman into the fast-flowing current, following the hedge-line upstream.

The brave horse forced his way through the flow, step by deliberate step, snorting anxiously, his ears swivelling to pick up Joe's constant reassurance: "Good lad, walk on, there's a good boy."

The water was still getting deeper, and there were no signs of life. It was hard to stay positive – easier to turn for home. But they'd come this far. They had to make sure . . .

Sherman began to walk more willingly, and the water retreated to just above his knees, then just below his knees. He gave a soft, high-pitched whinny – a funny sound to hear from a large, masculine horse.

Dark shapes, even darker than the water, were ahead of them. Joe peered into the blackness, trying his best to hold the torch steady. "Yes! It's them!" he shouted.

The five horses stood together, dejected and immobile.

Joe rode right up to them, bent down and put on their head collars.

They were shaking uncontrollably and hardly seemed to notice him. It was obvious they'd never move of their own accord. They'd have to be coaxed somehow.

Joe felt amazingly calm. There was a job to do and it was up to him to get it right. It was rather like the focused determination he felt as soon as he started a race. He manoeuvred Sherman between the horses, gathering up the lead ropes over their necks. "Caroline, can you lead Fortune? Then if you take Lightning, Emily, I'll tie Lady and ET to Sherman's hames so I've got a hand free for leading Kite . . . Drop the ropes if they won't move. Okay? Otherwise you might get pulled backwards. Walk on, Sherman."

Sherman walked. The ropes strained taut and then gave slightly as the horses followed in a daze, allowing the big, powerful horse to drag them along. He seemed to realise the importance of his job as he carefully picked his way through the turbulent water to the opening and then set a course for home, plodding on until he was asked to stop, leading his friends to safety.

Chapter 19

Six Weeks Later

Sunshine highlighted the colours of autumn in the fields and hedgerows. At first glance the scene looked idyllic, yet there were still tell-tale signs that the land had been flooded recently: muddy patches, broken fences and debris trapped in hedges.

The fields had recovered well, on the whole, but Mum's garden had been ruined. She hardly had time for gardening now, anyway, so she'd decided to plough it up and return it to grass. After all, they needed all the paddocks they could get.

Push on the left to go right and the right to go left, Joe reminded himself, taking hold of the plough handles. He took a deep breath and focused on the stick Malc had planted in the end hedge. "Walk on," he commanded.

The horses stepped forwards: Velvet on the left and Sherman on the right – land horse and furrow horse – perfectly in tune with each other.

"That's good! Keep a little bit of tension in those plough lines to let them know you're with them," Malc called. Joe gripped the handles and tried to adjust the thin ropes running through his hands as he walked along, wondering whether he'd got too much tension or too little.

"Stand up straight – don't slump!" Malc called. "Look where you're going, not down at the ground the whole time." There was a pause. "And relax, boy! Enjoy it."

Turning was the trickiest part, but even that became easier after a while. As Joe relaxed the plough seemed to relax too, running through the thick, loamy soil almost by itself.

Two years ago he'd dug some of this field by hand, and found the wishing shoe that he'd kept under his bed. It wasn't there any more. He'd taken out the wishes and it had joined his growing collection of horseshoes – reminders of the horses that had turned his life around: Lady's shoe, the shoes with rolled toes and raised heels that Lightning had arrived wearing, Treacle's shoe, a racing plate worn by Chocolate Buttons, the Scottish shoes Fortune had worn when she won the Prince Philip Cup, one of Solo's and a set of shoes from both Velvet and Sherman.

They were approaching the mark at the edge of the field. *Now concentrate* . . . Joe pushed down on the right handle to take the share out of work, kept the horses walking forwards and then made the turn: "Come round! Good lad, good girl." Hurray, much better.

If he found another shoe now, what would he wish for? That things would carry on going well between him and Caroline, of course, and also that the Bellsham Vale team would win the Prince Philip Cup in a couple of weeks' time. What else? No more floods – yes, definitely. Otherwise, he couldn't think of anything else he wanted, other than grand, impossible things like stopping all cruelty towards horses. Perhaps they were helping a tiny bit, though, by taking in rescue horses at the Hidden Horseshoe . . .

Had the other wishes really made a difference, or was it his imagination? Rusty, friends, Fortune and even the England team: would all those things have happened anyway? He remembered Nellie saying that the more help wishes got the better they turned out.

Perhaps it was a clever way of saying the wishing shoe had given him the confidence to make things work out . . . Funny he should start thinking about it here, because this was pretty well exactly where he'd found the shoe in the first place.

Phew, it was a pity they hadn't had this sort of weather in the summer. The sun shining on the plough was so bright. Odd how the soil polished everything – even the shoes on the horses were glinting . . .

"Woah!" Joe said. "Stand."

"What's up?" Chris asked, hurrying over. Malc followed him more slowly.

"I think Sherman's lost a shoe. Near fore," Joe said.

Chris went to take a look. "Yes, afraid so. What a pity – that's the one you made." He walked back along the furrow, searching for it. "Nope. I think you must have ploughed it in. Sorry."

Joe smiled. "Never mind."

He thought of the shoe he'd made, buried under the earth. Perhaps someone else would find it. Maybe they would wonder about the person who'd made it and the horse who'd once worn it. Maybe they would even notice it had seven holes and make it into a wishing shoe . . .

Only time would tell.

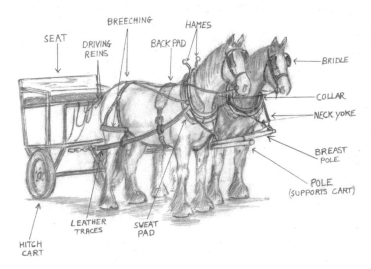

American Pairs Harness

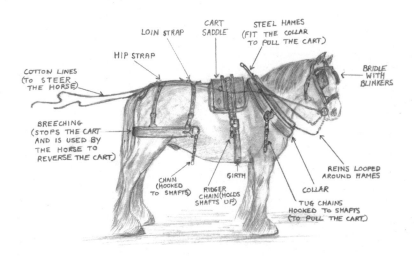

English Shaft Harness for Pulling a Farm Cart

Author's Notes

As always, I would like to thank my husband, Chris, for his support, his illustrations and for the horses he's shared with me over the years. When I'm writing he has to cope with odd meals, or no meals at all, and a preoccupied wife who locks herself in the farm office for hours on end.

Readers often ask me where my ideas come from, and the answer is "life". I'm often inspired by things I've experienced, read about or seen on TV, an overheard conversation, places I've visited or people and animals I've encountered. For instance, when I was growing up some good friends lived at a farm called Newbridge Farm, which was near Romney Marsh and prone to flooding, and my memory of it was revived by recent scenes of flooding on the TV. A news story about a herd of horses rescued from a flood was particularly useful.

We have kept heavy horses (Shires and Clydesdales) at our farm for the past twenty-five years, and for twenty years we ran a horse-drawn tour business over Exmoor. Both Chris and I love heavy horses, and so I was keen to include them in this story. We now have just one Shire horse in retirement at the farm. He was the mainstay of our horse-drawn tour business for a long time, and he's called Sherman.

Horses and ponies I've known often make an appearance in my stories. Sherman has already been mentioned, and there are others. We had a lovely chestnut horse called Tyler who was fantastic to ride but very aggressive towards people he didn't know if they came near his stable. One day he attacked a visitor to our farm. At the time we were running horse-drawn tours and self-catering holidays, so we couldn't risk him attacking anyone again and we made the difficult decision to give him away to a knowledgeable home. Oh, and I had to mention our lovely riding horse, Keep in Tempo. (I'm sure he didn't mind me turning him into the thoroughbred stallion who sired Kite!)

Beetle, our sheepdog, *hates* loud bangs – whether they're caused by guns, fireworks or thunder and lightning – so I had him in mind when I decided that Rusty was afraid of thunder storms.

Although we worked horses for many years, we've never ploughed with them, so I am indebted to our good friends Jonathan and Fiona Waterer, and also Will and Ann Williams, for their help with the ploughing scenes.

The Bellsham Vale Pony Club is a figment of my imagination, but the other Pony Club branches mentioned in this story are real – as are the mounted games competitions, including the DAKS International Pony Club Mounted Games Competition at Royal Windsor Horse Show. Many thanks, again, to the Capel family for their help with the mounted games information in this book, especially to Rory Capel who gave me a first-hand description of riding for England at Windsor. Another Devon and Somerset Pony Club member, Patrick Crane, rode for England when the team won the competition a few years ago, and he gave me a really useful account of what it was like.

This story originally included more about Martin's passion, fly-fishing, but unfortunately some of the fishing scenes had to be cut in the final version, so I apologise to Nick Hart for that. Nick teaches fly-fishing and has a fishing shop on Exmoor, and he provided me with lots of fascinating information, including some unbelievable names for flies!

Mark Rashid is an American horse trainer who has written some excellent books about his experiences helping all sorts of horses and horse owners. I was lucky enough to go to one of his clinics when he visited England a few years ago. He also teaches aikido, applies many of the principles of aikido to horsemanship and runs aikido courses for horsemen and women. A friend, Caroline Fardell, has been on one of his courses and said it completely changed her relationships with horses and humans, especially her understanding of feel and softness. Mark's ideas have really struck a chord with me, and I have found them useful when handling our own horses, especially our free-living Exmoor ponies.

Andrew Medland, instructor at the Shudokan Black Belt Academy, kindly allowed me to observe some of his lessons when he was teaching in Barnstaple, and he lent me several books about aikido, for which I am very grateful.

There is a strong theme of farriery throughout this trilogy. Our farrier, Clive Ley, and his assistants, Josh, Dusty and Jordan put up with me watching them at work, taking photos and asking endless questions about horseshoes and shoeing. Josh made a Shire horse shoe for me from scratch, like Joe does in this story, and Jordan filmed it. You can see edited highlights on YouTube. A link can be found on my website www.victoriaeveleigh.co.uk.

I'm also very grateful to Nic Barker, our local "barefoot farrier" for sharing so much information with me about horse hoof rehabilitation and keeping horses unshod. She suggested a scenario for Lightning's recovery from apparently incurable lameness, based on her experiences with many similar cases. After I'd written *Joe and the Hidden Horseshoe* I was interested to hear that the Capels used to have a talented games pony that became lame when shod but was fine when ridden barefoot.

Finally, many thanks to Fiona Kennedy and Felicity Johnston, my editors at Orion Children's Books, for giving me a perfect combination of freedom, guidance and encouragement.

Victoria Eveleigh
North Devon
September 2013

If you have enjoyed Joe's story,
you'll also love

Katy's Wild Foal.

Here is a preview of the opening.

1

Born on the Moor

Katy sat alone at the kitchen table, staring blankly at the birthday presents in front of her. A cheerful weather man on the TV was forecasting snow on high ground. Katy knew it was the last thing they needed at lambing time, but a part of her longed for the excitement of snow.

My birthday will always be in the middle of lambing, she thought gloomily. Why couldn't I have been born in the summer? Even Christmas Day would have been better than the first day of April.

Lambing was a hectic time of year at Barton Farm,

so Katy's family were too busy to organise a party or an outing somewhere for her. Today they'd done their best, she had to admit. They'd even said she could invite someone over for the day, but she hadn't been sure who to ask. She didn't really have a best friend.

Gran and Granfer had come round for the afternoon, so that had been fun. She'd helped Gran make a trifle. Everyone had stopped for tea, complete with trifle and cake. For a moment it had felt like a proper birthday.

Now it was early evening. Gran and Granfer had gone back home, and Mum, Dad and Katy's older brother, Tom, had gone outside to catch up on all the work that needed to be done before darkness fell. The house felt cold and empty.

Katy took the iPod her parents had given her out of its box. She'd have to ask Tom to set it up for her when he came in again, as the instructions were impossible to understand. What she'd really wanted was a mobile phone – everyone at school had one, except her. But her parents said mobiles were a waste of money because there was no signal at Barton Farm. Katy put the iPod back in its box, looked briefly at a jewellery-making kit Auntie Rachel had given her and then picked up an old book called *Moorland Mousie*. She turned the thick, yellowing pages. There were some lovely illustrations, but the writing looked rather heavy going. She found reading hard work.

"Take care of this book. I hope you'll love it as much as I did at your age," Granfer had said when he'd given it to her.

"What's it about, Granfer?" she'd asked, thumbing through the pages.

"It's the life story of an Exmoor pony called Mousie. A bit like the story of Black Beauty, but much better in my opinion," Granfer had replied. "That book started my lifelong interest in Exmoor ponies."

"Have Exmoors been at Barton forever?"

"Well, I don't know about forever," he'd said, smiling. "But they've been here for as long as I can remember, and way before that I expect. Your great grandfather was a founding member of the Exmoor Pony Society, you know. Loved his Exmoors, he did, and he was determined they should stay as they've always been. He was even against me having one to ride when I was a boy. 'Their place is on the moor, living as nature intended,' he used to say. Free-living, it's called nowadays. It means they live like wild ponies but they're actually owned and managed by someone, so they're not truly wild – not like deer, foxes and other wildlife."

The Barton herd of registered Exmoor ponies was one of the oldest and best herds in the country, and Granfer was a highly respected member of the Exmoor Pony Society. It was a great sadness to him that his son, Katy's father, had no interest in the herd. The farm had been handed over to Dad, but Granfer still owned the ponies.

Gran and Granfer had lived at the farm until last year, but Gran couldn't cope with the stairs anymore so they'd moved to a bungalow. Now they only visited a couple of times a week, and Katy missed them terribly. Barton Farm was an isolated place, surrounded by the high moors, several miles from the nearest town. She often felt lonely and cut off from other people her own age. Most of the children at school lived in town, and the girls were mainly into fashion and music, which really didn't interest her much, although she'd learned to pretend it did. Tom was nine years older than she was, and all he talked about was farming. He seemed to know exactly what he was going to do with his life: he'd go to agricultural college and then help Dad farm Barton. One day the farm would be his.

Katy put the book down and picked up the jewellery kit. The box slipped out of her hand as she tried to open it, and hundreds of beads and fake jewels spilled out.

"Oh, no!" she squeaked, watching in disbelief as they hit the floor and sprayed out in all directions like a multi-coloured firework.

What do I do now? I'll lose them completely if I use the vacuum cleaner. I'd better find a dustpan and brush, she thought.

The beads were surprisingly slippery. Katy nearly fell several times as she tried her best to gather them together. They seemed to have other ideas, shooting off in all directions as soon as the brush touched them. Eventually she managed to round most of them up and crammed a rather unpleasant mixture of beads, jewels, dust and dog hairs back into the box.

I can't face sorting it all out now, she thought. I may as well walk up to the lambing shed and see if I can help. The orphan lambs will need feeding soon. I'll go and give them a birthday cuddle. Perhaps they'd like a little bit of cake.

Katy took a piece of birthday cake, wrapped it in some foil and put it in the pocket of Tom's old army jacket which was hanging on the back of the chair. The jacket smelt overpoweringly of sheep and was far too big for her, but she put it on anyway. It saved having to hunt around for her own coat, and wearing Tom's clothes made her feel like a proper farmer. She went to the hallway, took off her cosy sheepskin boots – a birthday present from Gran – and winced as she slipped her bare feet into her chilly, damp wellies.

Socks really would have been a good idea, she said to herself. Oh well, too late now. I won't be outside for long, anyway.

She opened the door and stepped out into the sleety rain. Behind her, the door slammed before she had a chance to turn and shut it herself.

Cold drops hit Katy's warm face. Going from warm and dry to cold and wet was always horrible. Screwing her face up against the weather, she trudged along the muddy track to the lambing shed, which was a beacon of light in the darkness.

Nobody was in the shed, but Katy noticed a ewe in the corner straining and grunting loudly. She didn't know what to do, so she decided to stay and keep an eye on things for a few minutes, hoping someone would come.

No one came, and no lamb came out of the ewe. As she stood there, Katy noticed a newborn lamb nearby who didn't seem to know who its mother was. One ewe kept butting it whenever it went near her, and two others weren't sure if it was theirs or not. The poor lamb looked so wet and bewildered. Perhaps its mother was the one trying to give birth in the corner. Above the roar of the wind, Katy thought she could hear the tractor in the direction of the Common, so she left the sanctuary of the shed and went to find help.

The wind in the fields was even stronger than it had been on the way up to the shed. It snatched Katy's breath away and made Tom's wet jacket slap against her body. Underfoot, the ground was uneven and slippery. To add to her discomfort, the rain started to trickle down into her wellies, surrounding her bare feet with ice-cold water. With every step she took, the combination of bare feet, water and rubber boot made a rude squelching noise which at any other time would have had Katy in fits of laughter.

She reached the Common gate, but there was still no sign of the tractor, although she thought she could hear the rumble of its engine. Perhaps it was only the wind she could hear.

The Common was a large area of moorland on which Barton Farm and other neighbouring farms had grazing rights for sheep, cattle and ponies. It was here that the Barton herd of Exmoor ponies lived all year round.

Katy leaned against the gate and peered through its bars.

Water ran in a shallow sheet off the saturated surface of the moor, forming tiny rivers in the sheep tracks and making ponds against the boundary walls. A wide stream flowed through the gateway where Katy stood. Beyond the gate, she could see the outline of her den – a dark grey shape against the lighter grey of the rainsoaked moor and cloud-laden sky.

The den was a group of gorse bushes that had grown together and had been eaten by sheep so that they formed a circular shelter with a hollowed-out middle. Katy had made it her own special place, and she'd spent many happy hours playing there.

She was just about to turn for home when she spotted something moving on one side of the den. It looked like the back half of an Exmoor pony, with its head and neck hidden from view in the circle of gorse. Katy remembered Granfer saying ponies sometimes left the herd if they were sick or foaling. She opened and closed the gate with difficulty, and walked up to the den. It was odd that, as she approached, the pony didn't move. Perhaps it was caught up or injured. When Katy was only a few steps away, the mare leaped backwards and started whinnying in a low, agitated voice.

"Oh!" gasped Katy.

A tiny foal's head poked out of the bushes, followed by four matchstick legs which shakily supported a skinny body. Its bony frame seemed to be shrinkwrapped in dark, wet skin, and it looked impossibly thin and fragile. The foal started to walk with wobbly steps towards Katy, and she was spellbound as it came right up to her. She reached out and just managed to touch its tiny forehead with her frozen fingertips before the mare whinnied anxiously and the foal realised its mistake and hurried away. In an instant, the magical moment was lost and the mare and foal had disappeared over the brow of the hill.

the

orion star

CALLING ALL GROWN-UPS!
Sign up for **the orion star** newsletter to
hear about your favourite authors and exclusive
competitions, plus details of how children
can join our 'Story Stars' review panel.

Sign up at:

www.orionbooks.co.uk/orionstar

Follow us 🐦 @the_orionstar
Find us 📘 facebook.com/TheOrionStar